I0623948

Table of Contents

Matteo Bandello

Romeo & Juliet

A New English Translation by

Michael Curtotti

ALDILA PRESS

Published by Aldila Press Pty Ltd, Canberra, 2023.

Front cover design: Peter Selgin
Copy and structural editing: Maria Scala
Book Description: Jessie Cunniffe

Forthcoming in the *Shakespeare Begins Series*

Cinthio's Othello
Bandello's Much Ado about Nothing
Cinthio's Measure for Measure
Bandello's Twelfth Night

Also from the pen of the Translator

Matteo Bandello, *Romeo and Juliet, A New English Translation by Michael Curtotti* (English only edition).
Luigi Capuana, *The Dragon, the Witch and the Daughters translated by Michael Curtotti*, Aldila Press 2023, 2022
Michael Curtotti, *Ten Lives Declaring Human Rights: From Bartolome de Las Casas to Martin Luther King Jr.*, Aldila Press 2023, 2020

For Ranjana

*"... quando gli venne veduta
una fuor di misura bellissima garzona
che egli non conosceva.
Questa infinitamente gli piacque
e giudicò che la più bella ed aggraziata giovane
non aveva veduta già mai.
Pareva a Romeo
quanto più intentamente la mirava
che tanto più le bellezze di quella
divenissero belle ..."*

Introduction

It is curious to find the soul of Italy in the heart of England, but so it is. For Shakespeare put it there.

The most desperate loves, the vilest deceptions, the most delightful cross-dressing dalliances, and the bitterest revenge– Shakespeare found them in Italian novellas and put them on the London stage. *Romeo and Juliet* is no exception.

As it happened, *Romeo and Juliet* had already been re-worked several times before it left Italy and made its way (through a French translation) to England.[1]

Matteo Bandello's version took that journey, and even though Shakespeare had poor French and English translations to work with, on stage, he made it shine so well that it is one of his most beloved plays. It has inspired many re-tellings, including on the big screen.

Indeed, it wasn't only his *Romeo and Juliet* that brought fame to Matteo Bandello in his own lifetime. His stories were translated across Europe, appearing in French, Spanish, and English. They were enormously popular, influencing many writers and playwrights after him, not least, Shakespeare. Bandello was one of many writers of the Renaissance period whose works have played an important part in creating the modern world in which we live.

This new translation of *Romeo and Juliet* brings the delightful story, as Matteo Bandello told it, to a world that still loves the tale of the two tragic lovers.

Bandello's style and storytelling are inspired by Giovanni Boccaccio's *Decameron,* but written two hundred years closer to our times. Bandello's writing is clear and delightful, but some of the Italian terms he uses are now considered literary and rarely appear in works published today. Although such terms are few, a glossary is provided at the end of this edition, explaining them. Readers interested in accessing Italian Renaissance literature and older works will find this useful in improving comprehension of these texts. Students of modern Italian will deepen their appreciation of Italy's rich literary heritage. The English text is both a gateway to the Italian text and useful to advancing English for students of the English language.

The idea of translating Matteo Bandello's *Romeo and Juliet* first came to me in 2022, during a trip to Italy.

For the first time, we were going to visit Verona. It seemed like a great idea to re-watch *Shakespeare in Love* on the flight over, in preparation for exploring the city. But it was a disappointing experience. By then I was aware of Bandello's work, and the longer I watched the movie, the more disappointed I became.

The movie is brilliant storytelling in its own right, but it leaves you believing that *Romeo and Juliet* is entirely Shakespeare's creation. This is simply not true. I would have been better off watching the movie on my way to London, rather than Italy.

Of course, *Romeo and Juliet* is not set in London, and the events, characters, and plots already existed in the original Italian stories that ultimately became the play. *Romeo and Juliet* makes the most sense in the real life setting of Verona (even if the story is likely to have been entirely fictional).

As I set to work translating Bandello's story, its words sank into my heart, and I have come to love it, just as much as I love the Shakespeare play. There are passages in Bandello that don't appear in Shakespeare. Romeo's heartbreakingly beautiful monologue, when he believed Juliet dead, is one such example. Nonetheless, almost the entire plot of Shakespeare's play comes from Bandello's version.

Bandello has his own delightful style. That style made his writing popular across Europe. He has, indeed, been described as the most important *novelliere* (storyteller) of the Renaissance, influencing writers such as Byron, Cervantes, Lope de la Vega, Stendhal and not least Shakespeare.[2] Bandello's writing deserves to be read and enjoyed in its own right.

INTRODUCTION

In reading Matteo Bandello's version, we can see why Shakespeare loved the story so much, and yet much was left behind in Italy. Verona is indeed *fair*, in Shakespeare's telling, yet it is an abstract notion. Having now visited Verona, I share the opinion that it is indeed one of Italy's most beautiful cities. With Bandello, who knew the city himself, we see Verona in its splendid setting of river and mountain and we walk Verona's streets and breathe its air. We encounter the place where Romeo struck the fatal blow that killed the enraged Tybalt. The church of San Francesco is still where Bandello places it. Verona is not an abstraction. It is real.

We enter Juliet's home (aged near eighteen in Bandello's version, and not nearing fourteen, as in Shakespeare) and see the world she came from—a world Bandello knew intimately, for he spent seven years in Verona and many years living in nearby Mantua, where Romeo takes refuge.

More strongly than in Shakespeare, in Bandello we see how the power of melancholy played such an important role in the lovers' doom. We witness the desperate but often misguided efforts of their friends to save them, which, in many cases, made things worse.

Yet, in reading Bandello's story, we also experience the delight of discovering more clearly the genius of Shakespeare's pen—as wordsmith and as playwright. Shakespeare creates an adaptation of his source material for the stage, and in doing so, he fashions his own beautiful language. In Shakespeare's hands, comic characters provide relief and Mercutio takes on a tragic and prophetic quality. As he is dying, Mercutio lays a curse on Romeo and Juliet three times. His words "a plague on both your houses" play out as the tragedy unfolds.

Tybalt's violent qualities are highlighted by Shakespeare in the opening scene and at the feast held by the Capulets where Tybalt is restrained from killing Romeo, there and then.

Time is compressed in Shakespeare, so that Juliet's father exclaims:

INTRODUCTION

All things that we ordained as festival,
Turn from their office to black funeral;[3]

Yet, in Bandello, both mother and father are fuller characters who would have saved their daughter, if they could.

It is perhaps useful to the reader to offer some notes on editorial choices made in this translation.

The characters of the story are already well known in English under their English names and have become part of the English language. In this translation, for example, Giulietta is Juliet, and Tebaldo is Tybalt. Even in one case, Shakespeare uses an entirely different name. Bandello's Pietro is named Balthasar in Shakespeare's version, while Shakespeare's Peter belongs to a different household and is not Bandello's Pietro. Using the Italian names of Bandello only introduces confusion and uncertainty in translation. Many of the names we know came through the French version that separates Shakespeare's English from Bandello's Italian. Thus "Montecchi" becomes "Montesches" in French and "Montagues"[4] in English. "Capelletti" becomes "Capelletz" and then "Capulets." The Prince "Bartolomeo della Scala," becomes "l'Escale" and then Prince Escalus.

A table is provided towards the end of this book mapping Bandello's character names against those which Shakespeare uses.

For readers familiar with Shakespeare, this translation is organized in acts that generally parallel those used by Shakespeare. This assists in comparing Shakespeare and Bandello's versions with one another. In addition, "scene breaks" are marked with an act number and a capital letter in square brackets, noting that sometimes scenes or parts of scenes are present in Shakespeare but absent in Bandello, or vice versa. A table in the appendices provides a guide to assist comparison between the Bandello and Shakespeare plots.

Many paragraph breaks have also been introduced. Such breaks help to bring out the meaning of the story. As modern readers, we have come to expect them. They were not present in printed versions of Bandello's novellas in accordance with printing conventions used at the time.

Bandello's dialogue style is very sparse, in the sense that it is often simply introduced as "and then he/she said." This style is retained.

Often dialogue is in long monologue form, and where this is the case, the monologue is also broken up into paragraphs to help the reader.

Finally, a word of acknowledgement of some previous translations. The versions Shakespeare had available to him are of poor quality, and as mentioned, only loosely faithful to Bandello's version. I have been assisted, from time to time, by consulting Percy Pinkerton's 1895 translation appearing in his *Matteo Bandello: Twelve Novels Selected and Done into English with a Memoir by the Author.* His translation, although admirable, does not seem to fully capture the depth of feeling of Bandello's language.

Another translation I referred to, and which the reader may wish to consult, is that of John Payne, whose *Novels of Bandello, Bishop of Agen,* collect all of Bandello's novellas. The Shakespearean style that Payne adopts is not justified by the original Italian text, and although also a very good translation, it makes for difficult reading for the modern reader, who is presented with a large vocabulary of terms and phrases long fallen out of use in English.

Such translators sometimes criticize the quality of Bandello's work. I cannot help feeling that it is driven by a desire to place Shakespeare on a higher pedestal. As Bandello says of Verona, Shakespeare does not need our help to establish his own excellence. I do not share their opinion of Bandello. His writing was enormously successful, as already noted.

INTRODUCTION

Bandello's *Romeo and Juliet* is a beautiful work in its own right. However, if you really want to see Shakespeare's genius, reading Bandello's version is a must. In reading this translation, you will not only enjoy discovering the tale of *Romeo and Juliet* in this wonderful form that preceded Shakespeare, but also you will draw much pleasure, as I have, in noting the ingenious way Shakespeare brought the story to the stage.

It is true that a great love inspired Shakespeare's *Romeo and Juliet*. But that love was not the love of a beautiful woman he knew in life. It was a love of beautiful literature.

If we still appreciate *Romeo and Juliet*, it is because by the time Shakespeare put it on stage, it had been refined by several generations of writers and had already traversed cultural barriers.

Romeo and Juliet continues to break through barriers of time and place. So let us turn to Bandello's version; as with Shakespeare, the scene begins with *two households alike in dignity*, in *fair Verona*.

INTRODUCTION

1 Shakespeare is generally believed to have primarily drawn on an English translation by Arthur Brooke published in 1562, which in turn is believed to have been primarily based on a French translation of Bandello's novella by Pierre Boaistuau published in 1559. On the title page of Brooke's translation it is simply said that it is "written first in Italian by Bandell, and now in English by Ar. Br." A fuller discussion of the origin of both Bandello's novella and Shakespeare's play is provided in the Afterword.

2 D. Maestri (ed), *M. Bandello Le Novelle,* Alessandria, Edizione del'Orso 1992-1996. See reference in Zanichelli Dizioniario Più at https://dizionaripiu.zanichelli.it/biblioteca-italiana/matteo-bandello-novelle-2/ accessed 29 May 2023.

3 See the Afterword for a further discussion of the origin of this juxtaposition, discovered by Dennis McCarthy in the writings of Sir Thomas North.

4 The surname "Montague" is also connected with Thomas North. See discussion in the Afterword.

MATTEO BANDELLO'S ROMEO AND JULIET

Prologue

Valiant Reader![5]

If the love I rightly bear for my native land does not deceive me, few among the cities of beautiful Italy boast a loveliness more fair than does Verona. A beauty as much from the crystal waters of its noble river, the Adige, which nearly divides it in two, as from the prosperity with which the abundant merchandise of Germany endows it. Enchanting vistas of bounteous hills and pleasant valleys adorn it, as do open meadows encompass it.

Many fountains of the most limpid, fresh, and generous water are at the convenience of the city. Four noble bridges span its river, and in its streets, a thousand venerable antiquities can be seen.

But my words have not been uttered to extol my native land, which can well declare its own praises and distinction. Rather, will I recount to you the piteous tale of the great misfortune which there befell two star-crossed[6] lovers.[7]

MATTEO BANDELLO'S ROMEO AND JULIET

Act One

[1A] In the days of the della Scala Lords, there were two houses of Verona, most renowned among those of wealth and noble birth: the Montagues and Capulets. Between them, whatever may have caused it, was a fierce and bloody enmity. From it arose many mischiefs, being each of them alike in power. And many Montagues and many Capulets died, as did their supporters; and more and more the hatred grew between them.

Prince Escalus[8] was then lord of Verona, and he had greatly strived to pacify these two houses, but never was there peace, so deeply was loathing rooted in their breasts.

Nevertheless, he restrained their excesses, so that though peace was absent, at least their mischief, which had so often brought men to death, was bridled. So much so that if they encountered each other, the youth gave way to the elders of the rival house.

*   *   *

[1B] After Christmas one year, when the balls began at which the masked dancers gather, Capulet, head of his family, hosted a marvelous ball to which he invited the finest nobles of the city, both men and women. And the greater part of the youth of the city were seen there, among whom was Romeo Montague, who was between twenty and twenty-one years of age;[9] the most handsome and courteous of all the youth of Verona. He was masked, and it already being night, he entered Capulet's home among the others.

At that time, Romeo found himself desperately in love with a certain gentlewoman: Rosaline.[10] For some two years, he had been besotted with her, seeking her out in church or wherever else she went. He followed her without cease, even though she had not deigned to grant him a single glance. He had written her many letters, and sent her messages, yet she was unyielding in her resolve and would not permit herself to bestow even a smile on the impassioned youth.

So deeply did her rejections afflict him that he could not bear the agony, and after endless laments, he resolved to abandon Verona for a year or more and travel about Italy to break his unbridled passions.

Overcome, yet again, by the fervent love he felt for her, and yet cursing himself for falling into such a foolish state, he utterly lacked the power to depart.

Sometimes he would tell himself:

"Is it not true that the more I love her, the more plainly, by a thousand tokens, she shows me that my affections are not dear to her?"

"Why do I follow her about wherever she goes, when my adoration of her does me no good? Isn't it better that I not go to church nor to any other place that she may be, so that perhaps, not seeing her, the fire that her lovely eyes enkindle and inflame in me, little by little, may be extinguished?"

But alas, all his thoughts proved vain. For it seemed that the more she demonstrated her unwillingness and the more his hope withered, the greater waxed the flame of his love for her. So that on days he did not see her, nothing seemed good to him.

As he pursued this love with ever greater constancy and fervor, some of his friends began to fear that it would entirely consume him. They wasted many a breath on him, lovingly counseled him and begging that he abandon his vain pursuit. Yet he paid as little heed to their admonitions and wise counsel as the lady took account of his existence.

Among Romeo's friends was his companion Benvolio,[11] who became greatly concerned that Romeo, without hope of success, was squandering the flower of his youth in pursuit of this lady. Among the many times he had spoken to him, he said:

"I love you like a brother, Romeo, and it grieves me to see you melt away like snow in the sun. All you do and spend is squandered without honor and profit, for you cannot bend her will and she will not love you. And what good does this endeavor do you, when indeed the more reluctant you find her, the more you strive in vain?"

"It is unbounded madness to pursue a thing, not difficult, but impossible. It is clear as the sun that she neither heeds you nor anything that pertains to you."

"She has, perhaps, some lover so dear and cherished that even for an emperor she would not abandon him."

"You are young, Romeo, and perhaps the most handsome youth to be found in our city. You are (and I am permitted to speak honestly) courteous, virtuous, amiable, and well versed in letters, a praiseworthy adornment for youth. And more, you find yourself the only beloved son of your father, whose fabulous wealth is known to high and low alike."

"And does he withhold his money, or rebuke you if you spend it as you please? He is a benefactor who labors for your comfort and leaves you free to do as you wish."

"Come, wake up, and see the error as plain as day before you. Remove the veil that blinds you, hiding the path you must take. Direct your spirit elsewhere and conquer a lady worthy of your love."

"Her rejection justly angers you, and that anger can do much more in the realms of love than love itself!"

"The festivals and masked balls are beginning throughout the land; go to all the feasts, and if, by chance, you see she who vainly you have served, cast her not a glance, but look into the mirror of the love which you have borne for her. No doubt you will find relief from the great suffering you bear. For just and reasonable anger will so burn in you that it will banish this unruly appetite, and set you free."

With many other words and reasonings that I do not here set down, his loyal friend urged Romeo to abandon the ill-omened pursuit.

Romeo listened patiently to all Benvolio had said and decided to put the wise advice into effect. So he began to frequent the festivals and wherever he found the unwilling lady, he never gave her a glance, but looked about for others to choose who might be fit for him, as if he were going to market to buy an outfit or a horse.

*   *   *

[1C] It happened in those days, as has been said, that Romeo, in masked disguise, attended the Capulet festival. And, even though there was little friendship with the Montagues, they were not offended.[12]

Romeo had been there for a good while, hidden by the mask, but then he lifted it from his face. At a corner of the hall he took his seat, and there he freely observed the entire hall, which illuminated by so many torches, was as if it were day.

All eyes turned to Romeo, especially the ladies, and all marveled that he so freely lingered in that house. However, as Romeo was not only handsome, but also most gentle and courteous, he was loved generally by all. And perhaps his presence there did not trouble his enemies as much as it might, had he been older.

Romeo drank in the beauty of the ladies at the ball, and this or that lady, more or less, would please him. In this manner, he entertained himself, without taking to the dance floor. Then a girl of surpassing beauty, whom he did not know, passed before his eyes.

The sight of her brought infinite delight and he thought her the most beautiful and gracious maiden he had ever seen. It seemed to Romeo that the more keenly he gazed upon her, the greater her beauty became and the more graceful her grace. He began to contemplate her with an adoring eye, not knowing how he could ever take his eyes from her. Feeling an unaccustomed joy at the sight of her, he resolved to do all he could to win her favor and her love.

So the love that he had carried for his former lady, vanquished by this new love, gave place to this bright new flame never to be extinguished except by death itself. Romeo, having entered this unknown labyrinth, not having the courage to learn who this maiden was, gazed at her adoringly, as if at a field for his eyes to graze.

Her slightest gestures absorbed him and he drank deeply of the sweet poison of love, praising within his heart every gesture and each part of that marvelous vision before him.

He was, as I have already said, seated at a corner, so that when the dancers took the floor, all passed before him.

Juliet (for such was the name of the maiden who so entranced Romeo) was the daughter of the master of the house and of the ball. Although she too, did not know Romeo, he seemed to her the most beautiful and graceful youth who could ever be found, and she marveled at the sight of him. She cast him sweet and furtive glances, and her heart filled with sweetness beyond words, and joy and pleasure in equal measure wrapped her being. She longed for Romeo to take to the dance floor, so that she might better see him and perhaps hear him speak, certain that as much sweetness would attend his voice as had the sight of him. Long she gazed at him without the pleasure of it ceasing, but he, all alone, remained seated, showing no intention of dancing.

All his attention was given to contemplating that beautiful girl, and she, in turn, had no thought but to catch sight of him. As they looked at one another in this way, their eyes sometimes meeting, the fiery rays of their vision combined together one with the other.[13]

Readily, they realized that each felt love for the other, so that each time their eyes would meet they were both overborne by loving sighs. And each had no other wish but to speak with the other and better discover the new fire aflame within them.

While they were lost in this contemplation, the ball was coming to an end and the dancers began the torch dance, which some call the dance of the cap.[14] A lady who was in the dance pulled Romeo from his seat and drew him into it, so he now attended to his duty. Having passed the torch to another lady, he came opposite Juliet, as the dance required. And he took her by the hand, to the inestimable pleasure of them both.

Juliet then stood between Romeo and another whose name was Mercutio,[15] the squint-eyed, who was a worldly gentleman most courteous and pleasing and well liked by all for his clever wit and for his amusing jests. He was always ready with some new story to bring the company to laughter, and without harming any other, he would entertain them. But whether it was winter or full summer, his hands were always frozen and colder than the coldest alpine ice. And no matter how much time he spent warming them at the fire, still cold they remained.

Juliet had Romeo on her left and Mercutio on her right. As soon as she felt her lover take her hand, perhaps hoping he might speak, she turned and smiled at him. With a tremor in her voice, she said:

"Blessed the day that has brought you to my side!" And so saying, she longingly pressed his hand.

The youth, who was quick of wit and by no means a fool, sweetly squeezed back on her hand and replied:

"My lady, what is this blessing that you give me?" gazing at her with eyes which cried out "have pity," he was in suspense for any word her lips might utter.

Then, laughing sweetly, she replied:

"Do not be astonished, gentle youth, that I bless your coming near, for Messer Mercutio with his ice-cold hand, has for a good long time, already frozen mine, and you mercifully, with your delicate hand, have warmed me.

Without hesitation, Romeo responded:

"My lady, in whatever way I might serve you, that service is to me most dear, and no other wish than serving you do I have in this world, so that blessed will I count myself if you would deign to command me as your least most servant."

"And truly I say, that though my hand warms yours, the fire of your lovely eyes has lit a fire within me. I assure you that if your aid comes not to me, so that I may bear so intense a flame, in a little while you will see me consumed entirely, becoming but a pile of ash."

Scarcely had he spoken these words than the torch dance ended. Juliet, whom love had also seized, sighing and squeezing yet again his hand, had no more time to respond, other than these words:

"Oh my, what can I tell you? If not, that I am far more yours, than you are mine."

As all departed the ball, Romeo hoped to see where the maiden might go, but soon he knew, beyond a doubt, that she was daughter to the master of the house. This he had confirmed also by one of his well-wishers[16] who enquired of many of the women there. This news was to him most unwelcome, holding it both perilous and near impossible to pursue the desired end of his love. But the wound was already open and love's poison had profusely penetrated within.

For her part, Juliet, too, was eager to know who this youth might be, who she felt had already entirely captured her. She called her old wet-nurse, and entering a room, she placed herself by the window to look down on the street, which was well illuminated by many torches. And she began to ask her who was this, who was so dressed, and who was that, who carried sword in hand, and who that other; and also she asked:

"Who was that handsome youth who held a mask in his hand?"

The good nurse, who knew almost everyone, gave her the names of this one and that, and recognizing Romeo perfectly well, told her who he was.

On hearing the surname Montague, the maiden was as one transfixed, despairing of ever having Romeo as her husband, because of the hateful enmity between their two families; although, no sign of her inner turmoil did she reveal.[17]

Act Two

[2A] She then went to bed, and little was she able to sleep that night, with varied thoughts turning in her mind; but abandon her love for Romeo, she neither would nor could, so fiercely did her feelings burn for him.

The surpassing beauty of her lover warred within her. Yet the more difficult and dangerous the thing seemed, and the more her hope faded, the more passionate became her desire. So, hard-pressed between contending thoughts, which on the one hand fortified her resolve to pursue her intent, but which on the other seemed to shut every way before her, she said to herself:

"Where do I let my ill-governed desires carry me? How do I know, fool that I am, that Romeo loves me?"

"Perhaps the words he spoke to me are those of a clever youth, said but to deceive me, to take from me something less than honorable. He would mock me and make of me a fallen woman, perhaps seeing in this a way to pursue the vendetta against his enemies, that day by day becomes crueler between our families."

"But his generosity of heart could not bear to deceive she who loves and adores him. If the face gives manifest intimations of the soul, his beauty is not so inconstant, that under it, such a ruthless and steely heart should dwell."

"Rather should I believe that from so courteous and beautiful a youth nothing should be expected but love, courtesy, and kindness."

"Now if truly, as I believe, he loves me and wishes to take me for his lawful wife, must I not reasonably fear that my father will never consent to such a union?"

"But who knows? Could it not be hoped by means of this union, that between our two families perpetual concord and peace would follow?"

"Often have I heard it said that through such marriages, not only between private citizens and gentle folk, but many times among the highest princes and kings between whom the cruelest wars raged, that a true peace and friendship that satisfied all followed thereon."

"Perhaps I will be she who, through this chance, will bring tranquility and peace between these two houses."

And with this thought fixed firmly in her mind, every time she saw Romeo pass by in her street, she smiled happily at him, from which he too drew great pleasure.

No less than in her, varied thoughts continuously warred in him: sometimes hope, then despair. Nevertheless, he would pass before his beloved's house, whether by night or day, at very great peril to himself. But the happy glances that Juliet sent him, more and more inflamed his passion, and drew him back to her door.

The windows of Juliet's room opened above a narrow lane, opposite which was a farm-shed. Romeo, walking along the main street, when he came to the head of her lane, would often see the maiden at her window. And each time he saw her, her face would light up with joy, telling him that she was more than willing to see him.

*　　*　　*

[2B] Often, at night, Romeo went to that lane and lingered there, both because that way was not frequented and also because standing by that window, he sometimes heard his beloved speaking.

One night, it happened that he was in that place, and whether Juliet heard him, or for some other reason, she opened her window. Romeo retreated into the farm-shed opposite, but not so quickly that Juliet failed to recognize him, for the moon with her clear brightness illuminated the scene.

She, being alone in her room, with sweet tenderness called to him and said:

"Romeo, what are you doing here alone so late at night? Alas for you, if you should be caught, what would become of you?"

"Don't you know the bitter hatred that reigns between yours and mine and how many are already dead? It is certain you would be cruelly slain, which would be to your loss, and dishonor would follow thereon for me."

"My lady," responded Romeo. "My love for you is the reason I am here at this hour and I have no doubt at all that if your people found me, they would seek to kill me. But for what my meager strength is worth, I would pay my due, and no matter how many swords are drawn against me, I would not die alone. If I must die in this venture of love, what better death could I wish for, than to die here near you?"

"That I should be the cause of the smallest stain to your honor can never be, for I would shed the last drop of my blood, to defend your spotless and radiant renown."

"But if love for me does as much within you, as love for you does within me, and if my life is as dear to you, as your life is dear to me, you will banish these objections and make me the happiest of living men."

"And what would you have me do?" asked Juliet.

"I would, that you would love me as I love you and allow me to join you in your room, so with greater comfort (and less peril) I could manifest the depth of my love and the bitter pain that I continuously suffer for you."

Somewhat annoyed and troubled at this, Juliet replied:

"Romeo, you know your love and I know mine, and I love you as much as anyone may love, perhaps more than is proper to my honor. But truly I say, if you think to have me outside the fitting bond of marriage, you are greatly mistaken and we will not see eye to eye."

"I know that if you come too often to this lane you could easily be caught by a wicked soul and never would I be happy after. In conclusion, if you wish to be mine as I wish forever to be yours, then you must take me for your wife in holy matrimony. And if you marry me, I shall be forever content to go with you to any place wherever you may please."

"If you imagine any other thing in your head, go about your business and leave me in peace."

Romeo, who wished for nothing else himself, hearing Juliet speak these words, filled with delight, and replied that this was all his heart's desire and that he would marry her whenever she wished and in whatever way she thought best.

"Now all is well," responded Juliet, "But so that our affairs be ordered as they should, I wish that we be married in the presence of the Reverend Friar Lawrence of Reggio, my spiritual guide, if he be willing to do so."

And to this they agreed, deciding that Romeo would the next day speak with the friar, since they were on friendly terms.

*   *   *

[2C] This friar was a Franciscan, a master of theology and a great sage,[18] and expert in many things. He was, moreover, a marvelous alchemist and practiced in the arts of magic. As the worthy friar wished to keep the good opinion of the people and safely practice the diversions that came to his mind, he was most cautious in his affairs. Whenever it might prove of benefit, he sought the patronage of some noble person of repute.

Among the many friends who favored him in Verona, was Romeo's father, who was a gentleman in good standing and well regarded by all, and who held the firm opinion that the friar was a most saintly man.

Romeo also loved the friar greatly, and was himself much beloved of the friar. For he knew the youth to be sensible and of a lively spirit.

Not only with the Montagues, but also with the Capulets, the friar maintained a close friendship. And in confession, he heard the greater part of the nobility of the city, both men and women.

Romeo, with Juliet's leave, and with her instructions in heart, departed from her and made his way home. When daylight came, he went to the church of San Francesco[19] and recounted to the friar his success in love and the decision reached with Juliet.

Friar Lawrence, having heard all this, promised to do all that Romeo wished, first because he could not deny him anything, and second because he convinced himself that through this means he could bring peace between the Capulets and Montagues. He also thought by this means to gain greater favor with the Prince, who greatly desired that these two houses be pacified to end the turmoil in his city.

*   *   *

[2D] And so, the two lovers awaited an opportunity to attend confession to give effect to that which they had planned. The first Sunday of Lent arrived and for greater safety in her affairs, Juliet decided to entrust her secret to her nurse who slept with her in her room. Taking the opportunity when it arose, she revealed the entire story of her love to the good nurse.

No matter how much the nurse scolded her and sought to dissuade the intended enterprise, no result did she attain. So she yielded to Juliet's will, who was so skilled of word that she induced the nurse to carry a letter to her Romeo.

Her lover, having read the words she'd written, found himself the happiest of men, for she had written that at five that evening she would be at her window opposite the farm-shed, and that he should come to speak with her, and bring with him a rope ladder.

Romeo had a faithful servant on whom he had many times relied and he had found him always quick and loyal. Having told him what he planned, he left the task of procuring the rope ladder to his care. All in order, at the determined hour, he set off with Balthasar[20] (for such was his servant's name) to the place where he found Juliet waiting for him.

As soon as she recognized him, she lowered a cord and pulled up the rope ladder to which it had been attached. With the help of her nurse who was with her, the rope was firmly secured to the window's bars, and she waited her lover's ascent.

He climbed up boldly, while Balthasar hid himself in the farm-shed opposite. Having climbed up to the window, the bars of which were so close and strongly set that only with difficulty could one pass a hand through it, Romeo began to speak with Juliet. Then having exchanged an amorous greeting, Juliet said to her lover:

"My lord, you are more dear to me than my very sight, and I asked you to come because I have agreed with my mother that we will go to confession next Friday at the hour when the sermon is given. Tell Friar Lawrence, so that he ready all that is needed."

Romeo responded that the friar was already prepared and willing to do all they wished. After speaking long together of their love one for the other, when the time came to depart, Romeo descended. Untying the rope from the cord and taking it with him, he departed with Balthasar.

Juliet was full of joy, and each hour until she should be wed to Romeo seemed to her a thousand years. For his part, Romeo, recounting all to his servant, was so overwhelmed with joy that he hardly knew himself.

*   *   *

[2E] When the Friday came, as had been arranged, Lady Capulet, who was Juliet's mother, taking her daughter and her ladies, went to the church of San Francesco, which was then within the citadel.[21] Having entered the church, they asked for Friar

16

Lawrence. He, prepared for their arrival, had already hidden Romeo in the confessional booth in his cell, and had locked him within.

Approaching, Lady Capulet said:

"Father, I have come at early hour to give my confession, and have also brought my daughter, Juliet, for I know that you will be busy all day with the many confessions of your flock."

The Friar replied: "In the name of God, be it so."

Blessing them, he passed into the convent and entered the confession box where Romeo was hidden. On the other side, Juliet was first to present herself to the friar for confession. Having entered and shut the door, she signaled to the friar her presence within. Removing the little grating, after they had exchanged fitting greetings, he said to Juliet:

"Daughter, as Romeo informs me, you are agreed to take him as your husband and he is disposed to take you as his wife. Are you still now both of this mind?"

The lovers replied that they wished for nothing else.

The friar, having heard the will of each of them, shared some remarks in praise of holy matrimony. He then uttered those words that are usually said to solemnize marriages according to the law of the church, whereupon Romeo gave the ring to his dear Juliet to the delight of them both.

They then agreed that the following night Romeo would visit her and they exchanged a kiss through the opening of the little window. Romeo cautiously left the confessional and the convent and, as happy as might be, went about his day.

The friar, returning the grating to its proper place in the window, so that none would notice that it had been removed, heard the confession of the happy maiden and then of her mother and of the other ladies.

MATTEO BANDELLO'S ROMEO AND JULIET

Act Three

[3A] The night and time arriving that they had fixed, Romeo went with Balthasar to a certain wall of the garden. Assisted by his servant, he scaled the wall and descended into the garden beyond, where he found his bride attended by her aged nurse.

The moment he saw Juliet, he went towards her with open arms. Juliet did the same, throwing her arms around his neck. For a long time they stood embracing each other. So great was its sweetness that she was overcome and could not say a word. It was the same for her ardent lover, it seeming to him that he had never felt greater pleasure than at that moment.

They then began to kiss each the other, to the infinite delight and inexpressible joy of both. Retiring to a sheltered corner of the garden, there on a bench they found, they passionately lay together and consummated their holy bond. And Romeo, being young and strong of constitution, and much in love, many times lay delightfully with his beautiful bride.

They agreed to meet again, and through this means, to find a way to induce Lord Capulet to make peace and union between their two families. Romeo, after kissing Juliet a thousand times, and sighing for her a thousand sighs, departed the garden full of joy, saying:

"What man in this world is happier than I? Who can compare themselves to me in love? What woman more beautiful and graceful than my Juliet, has ever lived?"

No less did Juliet hold herself fortunate and blessed. It seemed to her impossible that any youth could equal Romeo in beauty, in gracious manners, in courtesy, in gentleness, and in a thousand gifts of person dear and beautiful.

Her greatest wish in all the world was that all be arranged so that with none suspecting, she could continue to enjoy her Romeo. And so it happened that on some days, the lovers found themselves together, and on others, they did not.

*   *   *

[3B] In the meantime, Friar Lawrence strove with all his might to foster peace between the Montagues and the Capulets. He had made considerable progress, to the point that he was hopeful he could obtain the blessings and satisfaction of the two families for the marriage of the lovers.

It was then Easter Sunday and it so happened that many of the Capulets had gathered on the main street near to Purser's Gate[22] towards the Old Castle.[23] Having encountered some of the Montagues, they drew their weapons and assaulted them fiercely.

Among the Capulets was Tybalt, Juliet's first cousin, a youth most valiant of character. He urged his companions to strike at the Montagues and to have regard for none.

The fighting quickly flamed hotter, as armed men first from this party then from that, came to the aid of their side. The combatants became so enraged that, heedless of any, many injuries were inflicted.

By chance, Romeo happened on the place. He had been walking about the city to pass the day with his servants and a number of his young companions.

Seeing his relatives at the mercy of the Capulets, he became greatly distressed. He knew the efforts that the friar had been making to establish peace, and knew that he would not wish for such a fray. To restore the peace, he cried out to his companions and servants, and his words were heard by many in the street:

"Brothers, let us enter the fray and seek by every means that this disorder not continue, and exert ourselves to make the combatants lay down their arms."

20

And so he began to beat down the swords, both of his own and of his opponents, and along with his companions, courageously with deeds and words, sought to bring the conflict to an end. But their efforts were in vain. The fury of the battle only waxed hotter, and the combatants paid no heed, except to laying blows upon each other.

Already two or three of each company had fallen to the ground. As Romeo sought in vain to pull back his side, Tybalt danced towards him, thrusting a strike at Romeo's side.[24] But because Romeo wore a coat of mail, he took no injury, for the sword could not pierce it. Then turning towards Tybalt, with friendly words he said:

"Tybalt, you greatly misunderstand if you believe that I have come here to quarrel with you or yours. By chance have I come upon you, and I have sought to remove mine own, wishing that we should henceforth live together as good neighbors. And so I beg and pray that you do the same with yours, that greater disorder not follow, for already too much blood is shed."

These words were heard by nearly everyone, but Tybalt, not understanding what Romeo had said, or pretending not to understand, retorted:

"O Traitor! You are dead!"

And in a fury, he swung a blow to strike upon his head. Romeo, who had sleeves of mail that he always wore, and about whose left arm was wound a cloak, raised it to protect his head. Turning the point of his sword towards his enemy, he ran it through his throat so that it passed from front to back, and instantly Tybalt fell face down to the ground, dead.

A great uproar broke out, and with the Prince's men arriving on the scene, the combatants fled this way and that.

Romeo was grieved beyond measure that he had killed Tybalt. Accompanied by many of his own, he fled to the church of San Francesco and sought refuge in the rooms of Friar Lawrence. The good friar, hearing of the events and of young Tybalt's death, was in desperation, concluding that nothing could now remove the enmity between the two families.[25]

The Capulets, united as a single body, went to lay their complaint to Prince Escalus.

For his part, the father of the now absconded Romeo, together with the leading Montagues, proved that Romeo had been walking about the city with his companions, and that by chance, he came upon the place where the Montagues were being attacked by the Capulets. In addition, Romeo had entered the fray to end the conflict and restore the peace, but wounded on his side by Tybalt, had implored him that he wished to retire his own and lay down arms. Nevertheless, Tybalt had returned to the attack, and matters fell out as they had.

So the parties argued hotly before the Prince, each casting blame on the other and seeking to excuse their own.

However, it being clear that the Capulets had been the aggressors in the fight, and proved by many trustworthy witnesses that which Romeo had first said to his companions and the words he had uttered to Tybalt, Prince Escalus ordered that all arms be sheathed, and that Romeo be banished.[26]

*   *   *

[3C] A great mourning for the death of their Tybalt arose in the Capulet household. Juliet's tears streamed profusely, and without cease. But it was not the death of her cousin that she mourned, but rather the end of all hope for reconciliation between their families. The sadness and misery of it infinitely tormented her, and she could not imagine how things might end.

Learning from Friar Lawrence where Romeo was to be found, she wrote him a letter full of her lamentations, and by the hand of her aged nurse, she sent it to the friar. She knew that Romeo was banished and that he must leave Verona, so she lovingly begged him that he find a way to take her with him.

Romeo wrote to her to be at peace, that with time he would attend to all, and that he still did not know where he would seek exile, but that it would be as nearby as possible. Also, that before he left, he would make every effort to meet with her, wherever might be most convenient.

She chose the garden where they had already consummated their marriage as least dangerous, and they agreed on the night and time when they should be together. Romeo, taking up his arms and accompanied by his loyal Balthasar, with the help of Friar Lawrence departed the convent and went to his wife.

As soon as he entered the garden, Juliet embraced him, all the while tears streaming from her eyes. For a long time they stood together, unable to utter a word, and as they kissed each other, they drank in each other's tears, which rained from each of them in great abundance. Consoling one the other, since they must be parted, they could only but weep and lament together at the ill fortune which opposed their love. Embracing and kissing, they lay together a number of times.

The hour approaching of their parting, Juliet, with most fervent pleading, begged her husband to take her with him where he willed.

"Sweet lord," she said, "I will cut my hair short and dress myself as a boy, and wherever it may please you to go, ever will I go with you and lovingly serve you. What more devoted servant could you wish for than I?[27] Oh, do me this mercy, dear husband, and let my destiny be bound to yours, so that whatever fate be yours, will also be mine."

As much as was within his power, with gentle words, Romeo sought to comfort and console her, assuring her that he firmly believed in a short time his banishment would be revoked. For the Prince had already given some hope of this to his father. When he took her with him, as she wished, she would not be dressed as a page, but as befitted her, as an honored lady, and as his wife and equal.

He said, moreover, that the banishment would not endure more than a year, for if peace was not restored by that time between their families, the Prince would intervene. Willing or not, he would compel a reconciliation. Come what may, if their separation still continued, he would find another path, for it would be unbearable to him to live so long without her.

They agreed to send each other any news by letter. Many other things did Romeo say to his wife to heal her heart, but Juliet was inconsolable and ceased not weeping. At last, with the dawn announcing the coming of the day, the two lovers kissed each other. Fiercely embracing, one the other, with sighs and tears, they bid each other to God's care. And so Romeo returned to San Francesco and Juliet to her room.

*   *   *

[3D] Two or three days later, Romeo left Verona, having already planned his secret departure, dressed as a foreign merchant. And he found good and trustworthy companions with whom he safely arrived in Mantua. There, he secured a house, his father making sure that he did not want for money, and he was kept in good and honorable company.

Juliet however, all day long, did nothing but sigh and weep, eating little and sleeping less, so that day and night became one to her.

Her mother, seeing her daughter weeping, many times asked her the reason for her sadness and what troubled her, telling her that, alas, it was past time to end her many tears, and that already she had wept too long for her cousin's death.

Juliet replied that she did not know what ailed her. Yet as soon as she could remove herself from the company of others, she gave herself over to her grief and tears. As a result, she became thin and deeply melancholy, so much so that she was almost unrecognizable as that beautiful Juliet that she had been before.

Romeo sought by letter to keep her close and comforted, ever offering hope that soon they would be together. He earnestly begged her to be happy and keep herself distracted, to not give way to so much melancholy, and to bear all things as best she could. But all in vain, for without Romeo, no remedy for her suffering could she find at all.

*   *   *

[3E] Her mother thought that her daughter's sadness (some among her friends having already married) was because she also longed for a husband. This thought having entered her head, she related it to her husband and said to him:

"Husband, our daughter lives a most sorrowful life, and she does nothing but weep and sigh. Whenever she might, she escapes any company. I have many times asked her the reason for her unhappiness and I have kept a close eye on her to discover its cause, and nothing at all have I uncovered."

"She always gives me the same reply, that she does not know her ailment. And all in the house shrug their shoulders and they know not what to make of it. Certainly, some great passion torments her, for so clearly has she become like a candle wasted by the flame."

"And after imagining a thousand things that it might be, only one has stuck there. I greatly fear that having seen all her friends becoming brides this last carnivale, and seeing that no word is said of giving her a husband, so has this sadness been born."

"This coming Saint Euphemia's Day she will pass her eighteenth birthday, so it seems to me, dear husband, in a word, that it is high time that you procure for her a good and honorable match so she is no longer unwed, for she is not the sort to be kept at home."

Capulet, having heard his wife and her words not seeming to him unreasonable, thus replied:

"Wife, as you have not been able to ferret out another cause for our daughter's melancholy, and as it seems to you that we should find for her a husband, I shall do all that seems to me fit to find her a decent match worthy of our house. But see if you can discover if she may be in love and learn from her which husband may most please her."

Lady Capulet said she would exercise all her wiles, and would not slacken in her enquiries, whether from her daughter or from others in their household, but nothing did she ever learn of it.

At this time, Count Paris of Lodrone, a youth aged twenty-four or twenty-five (most rich and handsome), came to the attention of Capulet. Pursuing this match with good hopes of a successful outcome, he informed his wife, and it seemed to her a most honorable and fitting match. She told her daughter, but the only result was that Juliet seemed more out of her wits with grief and sadness than ever. Lady Capulet seeing this, found herself exasperated, unable to fathom the reason. And after having many times reasoned with Juliet, she said:

"So, my daughter, what I am hearing is that you do not want a husband."

"I have no wish whatever to be married," she responded to her mother, adding that if she loved her and cared for her at all, she would not again speak to her of any husband.

Her mother, hearing her daughter's reply, said:

"What do you wish for then, if you do not want a husband? Do you want to become an old maid or a nun? Oh, tell me what is in your heart."

Juliet replied that she wished neither to be spinster nor nun, but that she did not know what she wanted, if not to die.

Juliet's reply left her mother both amazed and full of sorrow, and she knew not what to think nor what to do. All who were in the household knew not what to make of it, but that Juliet, ever since her cousin's death, had been in the worst of ways, and never ceased weeping. From that day on, she was not once seen at her window.

Lady Capulet shared all these things with her husband, who called for his daughter, and after several discussions with her, said:

"Daughter, seeing that you are, after all, of an age to have a husband, I have found you a groom who is noble, rich, and handsome. He is the Lord and Count of Lodrone. So prepare yourself to take him and do my will, for such honorable matches are rare to find."

To this Juliet forthrightly replied, with feeling greater than was becoming to a daughter, that she had no intention of marrying.

Her father became most disturbed and angry, coming close to striking her. But he only threatened her sternly with bitter words, concluding that whether she willed it or not, in three or four days she should resolve to go with her mother and family to Villafranca, because Count Paris would be there with his companions to meet her. She should raise neither quibble nor make protest if she did not wish him to beat her black and blue, and make her the most miserable girl who ever lived.

What passed through Juliet's heart, what thoughts, only those who have dared the flames of love, will know. She was truly like one struck dumb by a bolt of thunder.

When later she had recovered herself, she wrote everything to Romeo, sending it by way of Friar Lawrence. Romeo wrote back to her to be of good cheer, for he would come soon to free her from her father's house and to take her to Mantua.

Nonetheless, against her will, she was taken to Villafranca, where her father had a beautiful estate. She went there with that same pleasure as is felt by those condemned to death as they go to be hung at the gallows.

Count Paris was there, who saw her at church during the mass, and although she was thin, pale and melancholy, she pleased him.

So he came to Verona, where, with Capulet, the marriage was agreed.

Juliet, too, returned to Verona, to whom her father said that her marriage to Count Paris was decided, urging her to take it in good spirits and to be happy.

Holding strong, she kept back those tears with which her eyes were filling, and to her father she made no reply.

Act Four

[4A] When it was later announced that the marriage would be held by mid-September, and finding no other succor in her desperate need, she thought to go herself to speak with Friar Lawrence for his advice as to how to free herself from the promised wedding.

The festival of the glorious Assumption of the Blessed Virgin, Mother of our Redeemer, approached, and Juliet taking this opportunity, found her mother and said:

"Mother, my dear, I neither know nor can imagine the cause of the fierce melancholy that so greatly afflicts me, for I have not been able to free myself of it since Tybalt's death. And it seems that I continue to go from bad to worse, nor can I find anything to heal me."

"So I thought during this blessed and holy Assumption festival to confess myself to the Virgin Mary, for she intercedes for us. Perhaps, by this means, I will recover somewhat from my suffering. What say you, dear mother?"

"Do you think that I should put into effect that which has come to me? Or if it seems to you that I should take another course, teach it to me, for I know not where my thoughts take me."

Lady Capulet, who was a good woman and very religious, strongly approved her daughter's declared intention, urging her to follow her plan, and commending her greatly for her resolution.

So together they went to San Francesco and called for Friar Lawrence. When he arrived and entered the confession box, Juliet entered from the other side, and facing him, thus spoke:

"Father, there is no person in the world who knows better than you what has passed between my husband and I, so there is no need that I retell it to you. You will recall reading the letter I sent you, that you then sent on to Romeo, in which I wrote that my father has promised me as wife to Count Paris of Lodrone."

"Romeo has replied that he will come and he will attend to all, but only God knows when."

"Now the situation is that they have concluded among themselves that, this coming month of September, the wedding will be held, and I will be taken there, whether I will or no."

"And as time flies quickly and I do not see a way to free myself from this Lodrone (who seems to me a thief[28] and assassin, for he wishes to steal the things of others), I have come here to seek your aid and counsel."

"I would not wish with this 'I will come and attend to all' that Romeo writes me, that I will be left entrapped. For I am Romeo's wife and have consummated our marriage, and with no other can I be but with him. But even if I could, I would not wish it, for to Romeo am I forever bound."

"I need now your counsel and your help. But listen to what I have planned to do. I ask, Father, that you help me obtain stockings, jacket, and other clothing for a page. Once so dressed, I can, late at night, or at an early hour of the morning, depart Verona, and none will recognize me. I shall go directly to Mantua and find refuge in the house of my Romeo."

The friar, hearing this poorly planned and fanciful scheme and not liking it at all, said:

"Daughter, you ought not put this idea into action, as it would bring great risk to you. You are too young and delicately raised, and could not bear the burdens of the journey, as you are not used to traveling on foot."

"And then you do not know the way and you would miss the road and wander about. As soon as your father discovers you are not at home, he would send his men to all the city's gates and to all the roads about it. Without a doubt, they would easily find you out."

"Then having been brought back home, your father would wish to discover the reason that you departed dressed as a man. I do not know how you could bear the threats that you would face and perhaps the beating that you would receive from your own to discover the truth of the matter. And while you would have done your all to be with Romeo, you would lose all hope of ever seeing him again."

Calmed by the all too likely conclusions of the friar, Juliet replied:

"Well then, Father, since my plan does not seem good to you and I accept what you say, advise me and teach me how to unravel this twisted knot in which I find myself so miserably entangled, so that with the least trouble I can be with Romeo."

"Come what may, without him I cannot live."

"And if you cannot help me in any other way, at least help me so that if I cannot be Romeo's, no one else shall have me."

"Romeo has told me that you are a great distiller of herbs and other things, and that you can distill a drink that in two hours, without inflicting the slightest pain, will kill a man. Give me enough of it to free me from the hands of this thieving count, if you are unable to reunite me with Romeo."

"Loving me as I know he does, he will console himself that I would rather die than fall, living, into the hands of another."

"You will then free me and all my house of a terrible shame. But if there is no other way to free me from this tempestuous sea where, in a battered and rudderless vessel, I now find myself, I promise you, on my faith, that I will take matters in my own hands. One night with a sharp blade I will be cruel against myself and cut the arteries of my neck. For I would rather die by my own hand, than betray my wedding vows to Romeo."

The friar was a master alchemist who, in his day, had traveled to many countries, delighting in experimentation and discovering many things. Above all, he knew the virtues of plants and minerals, and he was one of the greatest distillers to be found in those days.

Among his concoctions, he compounded certain pure sleeping agents together, and made a paste of them, which he then ground to the finest powder of a marvelous virtue. If it were taken with a little water, in one or two quarter hours, he who had drunk it would sleep, and it would so silence his spirit that there was no physician, no matter how skilled or well practiced, who would not judge him dead.

The drinker of it would, in this gentle death, then persist for forty hours, and sometimes more, depending on the quantity that he had consumed and the constitution and temperament of the body which took it. The powder's work complete, the man or woman would awake, as if they had taken no more nor less than a long and restful sleep. No other disorder or harm would they incur.

The friar, being in no doubt of the fixed resolve of the desolate young woman, and moved to pity for her sake, struggled to hold back the tears which started in his eyes. With compassionate voice, he said:

"Look, dear Juliet, you must not speak of dying, for I promise you that if you die, you will never return here, if not on the Day of Judgement, when with all the dead we will be resurrected."

"I wish instead, that you resolve to live for so long as it pleases God. He has given us life and will keep it for us, and when he wishes he will call it back unto himself. You must drive out all these melancholy thoughts. You are young and now you must take delight in life and enjoy the company of your Romeo. We will find a remedy for all. Do not doubt it."

"As you know, I am, in this magnificent city, held by all in good esteem and reputation. If it were known that I was cognizant of your marriage, I should incur great shame and disgrace. But how would it be, if I were to give you poison? I do not have it. And if I did, I would not give it to you, because it would be a mortal sin before God, and I would lose the respect of all."

"You are well aware that rarely are even ordinary things done without my office being called, and that it is not fifteen days since Prince Escalus entrusted a task of great moment to my care. So, Juliet, for you and for your Romeo, with all my heart for your sakes, I will exert myself so that you shall escape this maze and be with your Romeo, and never with this Count Paris. Nor ought you die."

"But it must be arranged so that this matter shall never be known. You will need to be brave and firm, and to do all that I ask of you, since it will not cause you the slightest harm. Hear then how it shall be done."

The friar showed his powder to the young woman, explaining the virtues it had, that he had many times employed it, and every time found it to be flawless.

"Daughter," said the friar, "this powder of mine is so effective and of such great worth that without the slightest harm to you it will make you sleep for as long as I have said. In that deep quiet in which you rest, if Galen, Hippocrates, Mesue, or Avicenna,[29] and the entire academy of the most excellent medics, who have been or who shall ever be, saw you and took your pulse, all of one voice they would pronounce you dead."

"And when your body has digested it, from that contrived sleep you will awake, so well and beautiful as you would from your morning bed arise. So, taking this draught on the coming of the dawn, in a little while you will fall asleep, and when the waking hour arrives, yours seeing that you sleep, will try to wake you and will be unable. You will be without pulse and as cold as ice."

"They will call doctors and relatives and, in short, all will believe you dead. So in the evening they will bury you and put you in the Capulet tomb. There, in pleasant sleep you will pass a night and day."

"Then, the following night, Romeo and I will come to bring you forth, for I will inform Romeo of all by letter. He will secretly spirit you away to Mantua and there keep you hidden until that blessed peace between yours and his is made, which heart and soul I will strive to secure."

"If you do not take this path, I do not know how else to help you. But mind, as I have said, you must keep this thing a secret and locked in your heart, otherwise it will undo all our plans–both yours and mine."

Juliet, who would have entered a fiery furnace to reach her Romeo, let alone a tomb, placed full confidence in the friar's words and without a further thought, agreed, and said:

"Father, I will do all that you have asked of me, putting myself in your hands. Have no fear that I may reveal this to any soul, for I will be most secret."

The friar hurried to his room and, folded in a paper, he brought Juliet enough powder to fill a spoon. Having taken the powder, and put it in her purse, she thanked Friar Lawrence profusely. He, who had great difficulty believing that such a young woman could be so confident and daring that she would let herself be sealed up in a tomb among the dead, said:

"Tell me, daughter, would you not be afraid of your cousin Tybalt, who was killed so recently, and who lies in the receptacle in which you will be placed, and who must by now emit a putrid stench?"

"Father," she replied, "have no fear."

"If I believed that by passing through the torments of hell I could find Romeo, no fear would I have of those everlasting flames."

"In the name of God, so be it then," said the friar.

* * *

[4B] When Juliet returned to her mother she was full of happiness, and as they were going home she said:

"Mother, most certainly, Friar Lawrence is a saintly man. His sweet ways and holy words have comforted me so well that he has near freed me from the terrible melancholy I suffered."-

"With regard to my ailment, he gave me a pious homily as fine as may be imagined."

Lady Capulet, seeing her daughter so much happier than she had been before and hearing what she said, was beside herself with the joy she felt at the contentment and solace of her daughter, and replied:

"Dearest daughter, may God bless you! I am so happy that you are recovering your happiness, and we are indebted to the holy friar. We must hold him dear and help him with our charity, as the convent is so poor and each day he prays to God on our behalf. Keep him often in your thoughts and send him some good gift."

From the cheerfulness that Juliet manifested, Lady Capulet truly believed that she was released from her melancholy, so she informed her husband and both of them were content and satisfied. All suspicion left them that she may have some other lover. As they still had not the slightest idea of the reason for their daughter's misery, they thought her cousin's death or some other strange affliction had caused her distress.

Indeed, because, in truth, she appeared to them a little too young to marry,[30] they would have kept her two or three years longer without a husband if they could have done it with honor. But arrangements with Count Paris were already so far advanced that it was not possible to undo that which had been agreed and fixed, without a scandal.

*   *   *

[4C] The day on which the nuptials were to take place was fixed, and Juliet was sumptuously arrayed in a splendid dress and precious gems. She showed herself willing and laughed and jested. Yet, each hour until the time fixed to drink the potion seemed to her a thousand years.

The night came, before the Sunday on which she was to be publicly wed. She, as young as she was, without a word to any, prepared a glass of water, and making sure that her nurse did not see her, put it by her bed.

Little if any sleep did she get that night. Warring thoughts tormented her soul. As the hour of the dawn approached when she should drink the potion, Tybalt appeared to her imagination, as she had seen him, with the blood dripping wound cut deep in his throat.

Recalling that she would be laid beside (if not upon) him, and that within that tomb there were other corpses and many naked bones, she felt a chill within her body, and the hairs of her body stood on end. Fear so oppressed her that she trembled as a leaf in the wind. An icy sweat spread over all her limbs, and it seemed to her that those corpses were little by little tearing her body in a thousand pieces. For a time, fear so gripped her that she did not know what she would do. Then, having somewhat recovered her courage, she said to herself:

"Oh my, what am I doing? Where will I allow myself to be taken? If by chance I wake before the friar and Romeo come, what shall become of me?"

"Would I be able to suffer the foulness that issues from Tybalt's rotting corpse, when in my home I can hardly stand any stench, no matter how slight it be?"

"Who knows, if not some serpent or a thousand worms are found in that sepulcher, which I fear so greatly, and which so much disgust me?"

"And as my heart does not have the courage to look on them, how can I bear to have them all around and touching me?"

"Have I not also heard it many times said that many fearful things have befallen of a night, not just in tombs but in churches[31] and cemeteries, too?"

With these fearful thoughts and imagining a thousand abominable things, she had almost resolved not to take the powder and came near to pouring it on the ground. And so she was lost in strange confused conceits, some urging her to take the draught, and others bringing a thousand dangerous things to mind.

Despite the fantasies that had tormented her during the night, as the dawn[32] began to lift its head above the balustrades of the orient, impelled by her fervent love for Romeo that dominated her soul, and having banished her fearful thoughts, in one fierce gulp, she drank down the potion. She lay back down and, in but a moment, was asleep.[33]

*   *   *

[4D] The nurse who slept with her, even though she knew that her young charge had little sleep, was unaware that she had taken the draught. And so she rose from the bed and went about her chores, as was her custom.

When the hour came to wake Juliet, the nurse returned to her chamber, calling to Juliet as she entered.

"Up, up, it is time to be awake."

Having opened the windows and seeing that Juliet did not move, and gave no sign of waking up, the nurse drew near, shook her and said:

"Up, up, sleepyhead, wake up."

But the good nurse's words fell on unhearing ears. She began to shake Juliet as strongly as she might, and then pulled her nose and pinched her, but all to no avail. For Juliet had so entrapped the vital spirit that the most horrid and deafening noises of the world, in all their sound and fury, would not have wakened her.

The poor nurse was greatly frightened, and seeing that Juliet responded no more no less than a corpse, she was certain that Juliet was dead. Beside herself with grief and pain, and with bitter cries, she ran to find Lady Capulet. Overwhelming grief impeding her words, and gasping through her tears, she was barely able to say:

"My lady, Juliet is dead."

With hurried steps, Lady Capulet, weeping all the way, rushed to find her daughter arrayed as you have heard. We need not ask if pain and bitter grief overwhelmed her.

Her heartbreaking laments rose to the heavens. At the sound of them, even stones would be moved to pity and the tiger, enraged at the loss of its own cubs, would soften.

The cries and tears of the mother and nurse were heard all about the house, causing all to run to discover what was amiss. The father came running, and finding his daughter colder than ice, let no emotion show on his face, yet the pain he felt brought him close to death himself.

Little by little news of the discovery spread throughout the entire city. Friends and relatives came, and as the multitude in the house increased, so, too, swelled the lamentations.

Immediately, the most esteemed doctors of the city were sent for, and they applied all the stratagems that they knew to be most appropriate and salutary in such cases. But all their art was of no avail. Hearing that for many days Juliet had done nothing but weep and sigh, they all shared the same opinion. Truly, overwhelming grief had killed her. At this, the ceaseless lamentations re-doubled, and throughout all Verona each and all were pained by such a bitter and unlooked for death.

But more than any other, her grieving mother's pain was greatest, and weeping bitterly, she would not take comfort from anyone. Three times while embracing her daughter, she fainted and seemed dead herself, so that pain was piled on pain and grief upon grief. About her were many ladies, all of whom did their best to comfort her.

She had so loosed the reins of grief that she was carried away by its power, and despair threatened to overwhelm her. When people spoke to her she did not understand, and did nought but sigh and weep. From hour to hour, her laments rose to the heavens and she tore at her hair like a wild thing.

Capulet, no less sorrowful than she, shed fewer tears to salve his grief, yet all the deeper was the sorrow within. For he so tenderly loved his daughter that his pain was great, but he knew better how to temper its excesses.

*   *   *

[4E] That morning, Friar Lawrence wrote a long letter to Romeo explaining the arrangement of the potion and what had followed, and that the next night he would draw Juliet forth from the sepulcher and bring her to his room. Accordingly, Romeo should find means to come to Verona in disguise, and that he would wait for him until midnight of the following day, after which matters would be disposed as they best thought fit.

The letter signed and sealed, he gave it to a trusted friar and most strictly commanded him to go that day to Mantua, find Romeo Montague, and to give to him the letter, and to no other person, whoever it might be.

The friar set off and arrived in Mantua at a goodly hour, dismounting at the Convent of San Francesco. Having secured his horse, he sought the Father Superior to seek from him a guide to accompany him about the city and help him with his task. However, he discovered that a little before his arrival, one the brothers of the convent had died and there was a suspicion it may be the plague. The commissioners of public health judged that the brother had, without a doubt, died of the plague, since a node considerably larger than an egg had been found in his groin. This was a certain and undeniable indication of that pestilent disease.

Just as the brother of Verona was inquiring for a guide, sergeants of the public health arrived. They commanded the Father Superior, by order of the Prince, under the severest penalties, and if he held the grace of the Lord of the city dear, to allow no person whatever to leave the convent.

The friar from Verona protested that he had just then arrived and had not had contact with anyone, but his words and protests were in vain. He had no choice but to remain there with the other brothers in the convent, so that he did not deliver that blessed letter to Romeo. Nor by any other means did he send him word. This was to cause great harm and tragedy, as you will hear by and by.[34]

*   *   *

[4F] In the meantime, solemn funeral rites were being prepared for Juliet,[35] who all believed dead. It was decided to hold these that same day, late in the evening. Balthasar, Romeo's servant, hearing it said that Juliet was dead, was full of dismay and consternation, and thought to go to Mantua. But he decided first to wait for the hour of Juliet's burial and see her taken within, to be able to tell his master that he had seen her dead. If it was then possible to leave Verona, he would ride by night and enter Mantua upon the opening of its gates.

It was then at a late hour, to the universal sorrow of all Verona, that the funeral bier with Juliet within was taken up, accompanied in full ceremony by the city's clerics and friars to San Francesco. Balthasar was so shaken by what he saw, and so overwhelmed by pity for his master, for he knew that Romeo loved only Juliet, that he did not think to visit Friar Lawrence and speak with him, as on other occasions. If he had gone to seek the friar, he would have learnt the story of the potion, and recounting it to Romeo, the tragedy that followed would not have come to pass.

Now, as he had seen Juliet in her bier and had recognized her beyond any doubt, he mounted his horse, and making good time he came to Villafranca where he rested his horse and slept a while. Awakening two hours before the dawn, he traveled on, and with the rising of the sun he entered Mantua, making his way to his master's lodgings.

But let us return to Verona.

Juliet, having been carried to the church, solemn requiems for the dead were sung for her sake, and as is the custom for such funerals, she was placed in the mausoleum at about the hour of midnight.

The tomb was dressed in marble and very large. It was located outside the church at the top the cemetery. On one side it was attached to another walled space that was also used to bury the dead. When a new body was brought, the bones of the one who had been buried there before were cast into that void. And high above the ground, the tomb was pierced by small air vents.

When the tomb was opened, Friar Lawrence immediately arranged for Tybalt's body to be shifted to the side. By nature, he had been very thin and in death had lost much blood, so he was little marked and had little reek.

Having had the tomb swept and cleaned, and having the responsibility of arranging Juliet's burial, as gently as he could, he laid her out, placing a little pillow beneath her head.

He then ordered that the tomb be sealed again.

Act Five

[5A] Balthasar having arrived at Romeo's house, found him still in bed. As soon as he saw Romeo before him, he was overwhelmed by unnumbered tears and sighs and was unable to utter a single word.[36] Romeo, greatly surprised (and misfortunes other than those that had occurred springing to his mind), said:

"Balthasar, what ails you? What news do you bring from Verona? How are my father and the rest of ours? Speak, do not keep me in suspense! What could have caused you such distress? Come, deliver your news, whatever it be."

Balthasar, at last getting the better of his pain, with faint voice and halting words, told him of Juliet's death: he had seen her carried to the tomb and it was said that overpowering grief had killed her.

At such agonizing and heartbreaking news, for a good while, Romeo was stunned and unable to speak.

Then, in a madness, Romeo leapt from his bed and said:

"Oh traitor Romeo, disloyal, perfidious and of all the ingrates, the most ungrateful!"

"It was not grief that killed your love, for sadness does not kill."

"No."

"For you were the pitiless rogue; you, the murderous fiend. You, it was, that caused her death."

"She wrote you that she would rather die than marry any other and begged you by any means to liberate her from her father's house."

"And you, blind, indolent, you lack-love, you miserable dog, you promised her you would go, that you would not fail and that she should be of good cheer."

"Instead, you indulged yourself from day to day, unable to steel yourself to do as she had begged."

"You stood by, hands in pockets, and Juliet is dead."

"Juliet is dead? And you still live?"

"Oh traitor!"

"How many times have you written her and with your very lips affirmed that without her you cannot live?"

"And yet, still, here you are."

"Where do you think she is?"

"She is there entombed within, wandering about waiting for you to follow her, and saying to herself: 'Ha, deceitful, false lover, and faithless husband, who knowing of my death still bears to live.' "

"Forgive me, forgive me, my dearest wife! For I confess my grievous sin."

"Forgive me that the pain beyond measure I feel is not enough to kill me."

"I will myself perform that duty which pain and sorrow should have accomplished."

"In spite of Death, who deigns not to take me, I will take death for myself."

So saying, he seized the sword that lay by his bed, and drawing it swiftly from its sheath, turned the blade towards his chest, placing its point above his heart.

But that good servant Balthasar was quicker than he, so that Romeo was unable to harm himself. In a moment, Balthasar had removed the weapon from his hand.

Then, uttering those words a faithful servant ought say to his master in such a case, Balthasar earnestly dissuaded him from such folly. And as best he could, he comforted him, urging him that he must live, for no mortal hand could bring help to Juliet, who now lay dead.

Yet, the cruel and unanticipated news had so deeply penetrated Romeo's heart that he became as frozen as marble, and his eyes would shed no tear. And whoever might have seen his face in that moment would have judged him a statue rather than a living man.

But it was not long before the tears began to fall in such abundance that it seemed as if a spring had opened in his eyes and that from it flowed a stream. The words, the tears, the sighs he uttered, would have moved to pity the most iron-bound and stony heart that ever beat in brutal breast.

As his inner pain began to find release, so brooding thoughts began to stir within Romeo's breast, and he fell prey to his bitter passions, giving way to malignant and desperate thoughts. He decided, his dear Juliet being dead, that he himself could in no way continue among the living.

But he neither revealed nor uttered this fearful resolution to anyone. Indeed, he veiled his thoughts, pretending otherwise, so that neither Balthasar, nor any other, should impede what his heart had resolved to put into effect.

He commanded Balthasar, who had been alone with him in the chamber, that he should say nothing to any person of his wife's death and that he breathe no word of the error of wishing to take his own life, into which he had almost fallen.

Then Romeo asked him to prepare two fresh horses, for they must go to Verona.

"It is my wish," he said, "that in a little while you depart without saying a word to anyone, and that when you arrive in Verona, you say nothing to my father of my coming."

"Search out such tools and irons as are needed to open the tomb where my wife is buried, and props to keep it open. For tonight I will arrive late in Verona and will come directly to the cottage you have behind our orchard. Then, between three and four of the morning, we shall go to the cemetery. For I wish to see my ill-fated wife once more, even as she lies in death."

"Then, at an early hour, with no one the wiser, I will depart Verona, and you will follow me a little later, and we will return here."

Shortly after, he sent Balthasar back to Verona.

With Balthasar departed, Romeo wrote a letter to his father. He begged his forgiveness, that without his blessings he had been married. He narrated in full his love, and the marriage that followed.

He begged his father then, most affectionately, to establish at the grave of Juliet (his daughter-in-law), a solemn requiem mass to be celebrated forever, which he should arrange from Romeo's income.

Romeo had certain possessions a dying aunt had left to him, who in her last will and testament had made him heir. From this inheritance, he also provided for Balthasar, so that he would be able to live comfortably, without being obliged to attend to the needs of others.

These two things he insistently pressed upon his father, affirming that these were his final wishes.

And because it had only been a few days since his aunt had died, he begged his father that the first fruits of his inheritance be gathered and given to the poor, for the sake of God.

The letter written and sealed, he rested it on his breast.

Taking then a vial full of the most potent poison, and dressing himself as a German,[37] he mounted his horse, letting those with whom he was staying understand that the next day he would return at an early hour, and that he did not wish anyone to accompany him.

*   *   *

[5B] Taking to the road with diligence,[38] at the hour of the *Ave Maria*, he entered Verona and immediately sought out Balthasar at his home, finding him there, prepared with all that had been asked of him.

Then, at about the fourth hour of the night, with such tools and irons as they thought necessary, they made their way towards the citadel, and not being challenged by any, they arrived at the cemetery of the church of San Francesco.[39]

Here, they found the tomb in which Juliet lay, and with their tools they deftly levered its cover, firmly wedging it open. Balthasar had, at Romeo's request, brought a small lantern, which some call "*ceca*" and others "*sorda*." Unveiled, it assisted them to open the tomb and ensure it remained fixed open.

Entering within, Romeo saw his dear wife, who, in truth, seemed dead. Immediately, Romeo fell down in a faint beside her, as if he himself were even more dead than she. For a time, the pain was such that he himself felt near death.

After recovering, he embraced his dear wife, kissing her many times while hot tears rained down his ashen face; his broken sobs preventing him from uttering a single word. Long he wept, and afterwards, spoke many words that would have moved to pity the most merciless hearts that have troubled this world.

In the end, having decided he no longer wished to live, he drew forth the little vial that he had brought with him. Placing it to his lips, in a single gulp, he drank down the poison within, sending it down his throat.

This done, he called for Balthasar, who waited by a corner of the cemetery, and told him to come up. When Balthasar had climbed up to the edge of the tomb, Romeo thus spoke to him:

"Here, Balthasar, is my wife, whom I loved and still do love, as you only in part do know. It was no more possible for me to live without her, than for a body to live without a soul. So I brought with me the serpent's water, which you know will kill a man in less than an hour."

"And most happily I have drunk it and willingly I go to lie beside she, whom while living, I loved so much."

"If it was not granted me in life to be together with her, at least in death I'll lie entombed beside her."

"See the vial that held the poison, and recall the man from Spoleto who gave it to me in Mantua, the one who had live asps and other serpents."

"May God, in his infinite goodness and mercy, forgive me."

"For I have not taken my life to offend Him, but rather to not linger here among the living, deprived of my dearest wife."

"And even though you see my eyes filled with tears, think not that I mourn my youthful death."

"My tears are rather for the pain I feel for her death, for she deserved to live a happier and more tranquil life."

"You will give this letter to my father, to whom I have written the wishes that I would see fulfilled after my death, both regarding this tomb and for my servants who are in Mantua."

"To you, dear Balthasar, who have always served me so faithfully, I have left such provision that you will never need to serve another."

"I am certain my father will faithfully fulfill what I have written to him."

"Now, away! I feel death near me. For already I sense the poison steal about my members and blocking up my veins."

"Close up the tomb and leave me here to die beside my lady."

Balthasar, due to the things already said, was so distressed that he felt the searing pain of it would burst his heart within his breast.

Many words he said to his master, but all in vain. For no one had a remedy for the fatal waters, and the poison had already diffused throughout his entire body.

Romeo took Juliet in his arms, showering her with kisses, and waited for his approaching and now inevitable doom, urging Balthasar again to leave and shut up the tomb.

*   *   *

[5C] It was at that moment that Juliet awoke,[40] the effect of the poison she had taken having been consumed within her body. Feeling herself being kissed, her first thought was that the friar having come to take her to his chambers, held her in his arms and, incited by a lustful appetite, was now kissing her, so she said:

"Friar Lawrence! Is this the faith that Romeo had in you? Get away from me."

Struggling to escape his arms, she opened her eyes and saw that she was in Romeo's arms, whom she easily recognized even though he was dressed as a German. So she said:

"Oh, you are here, my love, my life! Where is Friar Lawrence? Why do you not take me forth from this tomb? Let us away, for the love of God!"

Romeo knew beyond doubt, as soon as he saw Juliet open her eyes and heard her speak, that she was living and not dead. He felt a burst of joy, yet pain beyond any that might be believed. Weeping, he embraced his dear wife, holding her tightly to his chest, saying:

"Oh life of my life and body of my body, what man in this world has ever had such joy as I in this moment, who believed you dead, yet now find that I hold you alive and well within my arms?"

"And what pain was ever equal to my pain and what unbearable penance can measure to my anguish? For I feel myself nearing the end of my wretched days and life slipping from me, when I should be delighting in life!"

"For my life can last no longer than a half hour. That it is all the time now left me."

"Has any being, in the self-same moment and the self-same heart, felt both the great joy and infinite pain, that I myself, now feel?"

"I am in bliss, and the fullness of the contentment and joy I feel is beyond expression, that beyond hope, I see you, my sweet bride, living, when I believed you dead and had so bitterly mourned you."

"And truly gentle wife, for such reasons, I must rejoice with you."

"But unmeasured grief and pain without equal overwhelm me, thinking that soon no more will it be granted me to see you, to hear you and to be yours, enjoying the blessing of your sweet company, for which I so much longed."

"It is true that the joy of seeing you alive before me is much greater than the pain that torments me. Yet the hour at which I must be parted from you draws near, and I pray our Lord God that the years that my ill-starred youth has lost, may be added to your own, and that He grants you a long life and that yours may be a happier fate, for already I feel my life ending."

Juliet, hearing Romeo's words, and having already returned somewhat to her senses, replied:

"What are these words, my lord, which you press upon my ears?"

"Is this the comfort you would give me?"

"Did you come here from Mantua, to bring such news? What is wrong with you?"

The ill-fated Romeo then told her of the poison he had drunk.

"Oh my, oh my," said Juliet, "What am I hearing? What are you saying?"

"Ah, woe is me!"

"Did not Friar Lawrence write to you of the plans that he and I made together, as he promised to do?"

The maiden, inconsolable and in bitter grief, weeping, crying out, sighing, was nearly driven to madness. She recounted in detail what she and the friar had arranged, so that she would not be compelled to marry the husband her father wished for her. Hearing this, the pain Romeo felt increased immeasurably, so that he could hardly bear it.

As Juliet fiercely blamed herself for their misfortunes and cried out to the heavens and the stars in their cruelest disposition, Romeo's eyes fell on Tybalt's corpse that lay nearby, whom he had killed some months earlier in the street battle, as you have already heard. Recognizing him, he turned to him saying:

"Tybalt, wherever you may be, you have to know that I had no wish to harm you. Indeed, I entered the fray to quieten it, warning you to withdraw with your own, and I told you that I would bring my own to lay down arms."

"But you, full of rage and ancient hatred, paid no heed to what I said, and with murderous spirit attacked me and drew forth the cruelty within me."

"I, provoked by you, losing self-restraint, became unwilling to retreat a step, and defending myself, it was your unhappy destiny that I should kill you."

"Now, I beg forgiveness for the injury I caused you, the more so that I had already become your kin, through your cousin, who was then my married wife."

"If you crave revenge against me, here, your wish is granted! What better revenge could you wish for, than to know that he who killed you has, by his own hand and in your presence, poisoned himself, and that he willingly dies before you, and will lay here buried next to you?"

"If in life, we fought each other, in death, in one tomb, without quarrel, we shall rest together."

Balthasar, hearing these heartrending words from the husband and the weeping of his wife, was as still as a marble statue, and knew not if what he saw and heard was real or was a dream. He was so stunned that he knew neither what to do, nor what to say.

Poor Juliet, more sorrowful than any woman and in immeasurable pain and sorrow, said to Romeo:

"As it did not please God that we should live together, may it at least please Him that I should rest here beside you. This you must know for certain, come what may, without you I will never depart."

Romeo, taking her again in his arms, began pleading and seeking to persuade her to take comfort, saying that she should go on living. For it would be a consolation to him to know that she remained among the living. And to this end he said many things.

Little by little, he felt his life departing, and already his sight was darkened, and the strength of his body so weakened, that he could no longer hold himself erect. Sinking to the ground, he looked piteously in the suffering face of his wife saying:

"Oh my beloved, I am dying."

*   *   *

[5D] Friar Lawrence,[41] whatever may have been the reason, had decided not to bring Juliet to his chamber the night that she was buried. The following night however, as Romeo had not appeared, he took a trusted friar, and with their tools and irons, they proceeded to the tomb, arriving just as Romeo was slipping to the ground.

Seeing the tomb open and recognizing Balthasar, he said:

"Hail Balthasar, where is Romeo?"

Juliet, hearing his voice and recognizing the friar, lifted her head, saying:

"May God forgive you, did you send the letter to Romeo?"

"I did send it," replied Friar Lawrence, "and Friar John delivered it, who is known to you. But why do you speak to me so?"

Weeping bitterly, Juliet replied:

"Climb up and you will see for yourself."

The friar ascended, and seeing Romeo laid out, with little life left in him, said:

"Romeo, my son, what ails you?"

Romeo, opening languid eyes, recognized the friar. Speaking softly, he said that he left Juliet to his care, and that for him there was no more remedy nor counsel. He repented of his sins towards him and God and sought forgiveness from them both.

Only with a great struggle had the unhappy lover been able to utter these last words. Striking himself feebly on the chest, he lost every strength, closed his eyes, and died.

How dreadful, how agonizing, how unbearable was his death to his inconsolable wife, that I have not heart to disclose it to you. But those who have known true love, think on it and imagine if you were to find yourself in such a horrid scene.

In misery at the afflictions that had befallen her, Juliet wept greatly, and many times in vain called out her lover's name. Overwhelmed by anguish, she fell senseless on the body of her husband, and remained there so a long while.

The friar and Balthasar, tormented by their grief, did all they could to revive her.

When she came to, she wrung her hands together, and with emotion and tears overwhelming her, she shed as many tears, as had any woman before her. Kissing her husband's dead body, she said:

"Sweet abode of all my thoughts and all the joys that I have ever lived. Dear and only lord, how bitter has your sweetness become to me!"

"In the flower of your youthful beauty and grace you have finished your race, taking no heed to care for the life that all held so high in their esteem."

"You wished to die, at an age when others hold life most dear, and having achieved your goal, you are now in that place where all, whether soon or late, will find their end."

"You came here, my lord, to end your days in the lap of she whom you loved above every other thing, and to whom you are the only beloved, she whom you believed dead and buried, and to whom you came willingly to lay beside in death."

"You never thought that your death would be to me the cause of bitter living tears."

"You did not think that going to the next world, you would not find me there."

"I am certain that not finding me, you have returned here to see if I follow behind you."

"Do I not feel your spirit here, wandering about? It departs and yet does it not marvel, suffer rather, that I still delay?"

"My lord, I see you, I hear you, I know you, and I know that you wait for nothing but that I join you."

"Fear not, my lord. Doubt not. For I would never wish to remain here, deprived of your company. Whatever may come, life without you would be more bitter and full of anguish than any kind of death man may imagine. Without you I cannot live, and even if it seemed to others that I were living, in truth, that life would be to me nothing but an endless and tortured dying."

"So, my dear husband, be sure. Soon will I come and abide with you forever."

"And in what better company could I depart this sorrowful and troubled life, and what could be more dear and faithful to me than following after you? Certainly, in my eyes, there is nothing better."[42]

The friar and Balthasar, who were at her side, overcome with endless compassion, wept. They used every means they could imagine in an effort to comfort her. But all in vain.

Friar Lawrence said to her:

"My daughter, some things done, can never be undone."

"If by tears, Romeo could be resurrected, we would all weep bitterly to bring him back to life. But there is no remedy."

"Take comfort and live, and if you do not wish to return to your home, let me find you a place in a holy nunnery, where, serving God you can pray for the soul of your Romeo."

But she had no wish at all to listen to such counsel, and persisted in her fierce resolve. She grieved that she could not, by giving her own life, restore that of Romeo's. Her only wish was death. Locking up her spirit within herself, with Romeo in her lap, without a further word, she died.

*   *   *

[5E] Now, while the two friars and Balthasar endeavored about the dead Juliet to revive her, believing her to have fainted, the officers of the law happened by. Seeing candles lit within the tomb, they came running.

Once they had arrived, they seized the brothers and Balthasar. Having understood the piteous case of the unfortunate lovers, and leaving the friars under a goodly guard, they took Balthasar to the Prince and reported to him how they had found him.

The Prince required that he be told in detail the entire story of the two lovers. By that time, the dawn having come, he arose, wishing to see the bodies of the two deceased.

News of these events spread throughout the entire city of Verona, so that both high and low gathered at the tomb.

The friars were pardoned, as was Balthasar.

To the unmeasured grief of both the Montagues and Capulets and all who called that city home, a funeral of great magnificence was held. And it was the Prince's will that the lovers rest there together in that same vault.

For this reason, the Montagues and Capulets made peace between themselves, although, indeed, it did not long endure.

Romeo's father, having read his son's letter, after the bitterest mourning, fulfilled entirely his son's parting wishes.

On the tomb of the two lovers, an epitaph was inscribed which said:

Romeo, convinced his bride most fair already dead,
    No longer willed to live,
    So his life, while lying in her lap, he took away,
    With viper's water (as men do call it).

As the dreadful news she learned,
    Weeping to her lord she turned,
    And pouring out all her grief,
    Cursed iniquity of Earth and Heaven.

Seeing then his life, O my, departing,
    More dead than he already, she said:
    "Oh God, grant me that my lord I follow,

This my sole desire, aim, and prayer,
    That wherever he may go, I may about him circle."
    And with these words, of overwhelming grief, she died.[43]

5 Bandello presents his novellas as a series of stories, which he heard told in various gatherings, and then set down in writing in his collection. Each story is prefaced with a brief description of the occasion of which Bandello claimed to have heard it. He is however following the convention of a fictional frame narrative found in collections such as Boccaccio's *The Decameron* and in *A Thousand and One Nights*. The story thus addresses "the Valiant Lord" in whose home the story is told. In our world, we might say "Valiant Reader," or "Valiant Listener."

6 Here, Romeo and Juliet are described as "star-crossed lovers;" these words are, of course, Shakespeare's.

7 Bandello here speaks with the voice of Captain Pellegrino, a native of Verona. See further discussion in the Afterword.

8 Prince Escalus or "Bartolomeo della Scala," is most likely based on the first Bartolomeo della Scala who ruled in Verona from 1301-1304, and who was also an important patron of Dante Alighieri.

9 Romeo's age is not mentioned in Shakespeare's play.

10 Bandello does not name the lady, but here "Rosaline" is provided as a reminder of Shakespeare's character derived from the character Bandello refers to only as "a gentlewoman."

11 The name Benvolio is not used by Matteo Bandello, but is employed for clarity for those familiar with Shakespeare, who applies this name to Romeo's young counsellor. See note 16.

[12] Shakespeare follows Brooke's version in which the Montagues were not welcome at the Feast. Then, to explain why Romeo was not expelled, Brooke introduces the idea that the Capulets did not wish to cause disturbance or offend the Prince. Shakespeare adapts this idea to further develop Tybalt's character as a hothead bent on violence, who is forced to put up his sword by Lord Capulet. This foreshadows Tybalt's later violence, which leads to his death.

[13] Bandello here seems to employ the "emission" theory of light which was held by ancient Greeks such as Plato, Euclid, and Galen. In this theory, light (or fiery rays), emerged from the eye, rather than as we understand it now, entering the eye. The emission theory was still being debated in medieval and early modern Europe, even though it had been decisively disproven by the Arabic polymath Ibn Al-Haytham centuries before. Bandello is perhaps using the theory for literary effect.

[14] The term used here is "torchio," which most authorities consider to be a torch or candle. The term "torchio" may also mean a flexible branch for tying a bundle of branches or wheat (although that does not seem to be the sense here).

[15] Bandello's character is called "Marcuccio" (a diminutive of Marco). In Shakespeare's version, Mercutio's wit is biting rather than sweet and courtly, and Mercutio's actions contribute to the death of Tybalt and the ensuing tragedy. Shakespeare establishes Mercutio's comic leaning through a long speech dedicated to the prankster fairy Queen Mab. There is no equivalent of this in Bandello.

[16] In the Italian word "benvogliente," which Bandello uses, we hear possibly a resonance of the character name Benvolio that Shakespeare uses in his play. An equivalent word does not appear in the French Boaistuau version of the story which Brooke translated into English. Nor does it appear in Da Porto's Italian text. It perhaps provides evidence that Shakespeare read Bandello's text.

17 Shakespeare fashions Juliet's anguish at Romeo's surname into some of the most famous lines he gives Juliet.

18 The term "filosofo," used here by Bandello in the early modern period, implied not only a knowledge of philosophy, but also of science.

19 The church of San Francesco is today, fittingly enough, on Via Shakespeare in Verona. Sadly the city does not celebrate the name of Matteo Bandello in any of its streets, although he is memorialized in cities such as Milan, Rome, Pavia, Reggio Emilia and Turin.

20 In Bandello's version, the name of Romeo's servant is "Pietro," however, Shakespeare applies the name Peter to a servant of Juliet's household. Here, Balthasar is used, as this is the name Shakespeare gives Romeo's servant. See the Afterword which further discusses this change.

21 The church of San Francesco was, in the era of Bandello, found in a square-walled citadel on the southeastern side of the city.

22 Porta dei Borsari. This ancient gate is still found in Verona. It was built in Roman times, when Verona was smaller and the city walls stood in a place which later was incorporated within the medieval city.

23 This would be on the street known today as Corso Cavour between the Castelvecchio Museum and the Porta dei Borsari, near the western edge of the old city of Verona.

24 Bandello here uses "stoccata," an Italian fencing term that does not appear in the English sources of the story available to Shakespeare. This and other Italian fencing terms Shakespeare uses in *Romeo and Juliet,* had however appeared in the 1590's in England in Vincentio Saviolo's fencing manual.

25 In Shakespeare, Romeo's killing of Tybalt is driven by rage and revenge for the death of Mercutio, rather than self-defense.

26 In Shakespeare's version, the Prince appears on the street where the fight occurred and the debate and banishment all occur in the same place.

27 Here the word "ragazzo," meaning "boy," is used figuratively for "page"– a younger male who attended to their master's needs–as we see in the text. Another example of this occurs in Bandello's story of Lattanzio and Nicuola, which is familiar in English literature in the form of Shakespeare's *Twelfth Night*.

28 Bandello employs a play on words, using the term "ladrone," which means "great thief" in Italian.

29 Galen and Hippocrates were ancient Greek physicians. Avicenna was the well-known medieval Persian polymath and physician. Mesue refers to Joannis Mesue or Yuhanna ibn Masawayh, a pharmacologist from Gondeshapur who lived in the eighth and ninth centuries. His works were famous and influential in medieval and early modern Europe. He was sometimes referred to as the "Prince of Medicine" or the "Divine Mesue". De Vos, Paula. "The 'Prince of Medicine': Yūḥannā ibn Māsawayh and the Foundations of the Western Pharmaceutical Tradition." *Isis* 104, no. 4 (2013): 667-712.

30 In Bandello, Juliet is aged eighteen. Although, earlier, her father said she is old enough to marry, even eighteen is identified here as too young. This detail is of interest. Curiously, for reasons best known to themselves, Brooke, who translated Boaistuau's French version into English, makes Juliet sixteen. Shakespeare makes her "not yet fourteen" (repeating the figure several times). The lowering of her age might have been due to Elizabethan prejudice towards presumed Italian cultural practices, or perhaps, was driven by the believability of the boy actor who would have played Juliet in Elizabethan England. In Italy of this era, women were already actors on stage.

31 In Italy, the church building itself was often a place of burial before the modern era.

32 Bandello uses the capitalized word "Aurora" which can mean "dawn" or can also allude to the Roman Goddess of the dawn of the same name.

33 Shakespeare's version provides an additional scene following this, in which preparations are made in the Capulet hall for the festivities. He then uses this device to heighten pathos when "celebration" becomes "mourning" and "marriage" immediately transitions to "funeral." See further the discussion in the Afterword.

34 In Shakespeare's version, this scene does not appear, but Friar Lawrence learns later that his message to Romeo has gone astray when his messenger returns to Verona (Act 5, Scene 2).

35 In Shakespeare's version, this scene continues from the mourning for Juliet's apparent death to her funeral in a single uninterrupted scene, without the switch to developments in Mantua.

36 This scene is substantially different in Bandello, containing a lengthy monologue by Romeo on hearing Juliet is dead, as he believes. In Shakespeare, this monologue has been lost. Instead, Romeo quickly dismisses Balthasar and finds an apothecary who gives him poison. Rather than dwelling on the pain and guilt he feels, Romeo's words, as given by Shakespeare, and the sources he relied on, dwell on the apothecary and the use of poison to achieve his own death.

37 The use of "German" in this context speaks to the frequent commerce and travel between Germany and Italy in this era, which passed through Verona. It was the route used centuries later by the poet Goethe in his travels to Italy. At the beginning of his story, Bandello notes the commerce that flowed up and down the Adige between Italy and Germany.

38 In Shakespeare's play, Act 5 Scene 2, Friar Lawrence learns that his message to Romeo has gone astray when his friar friend returns to Verona and informs him accordingly. It also contains the plot element concerning the plague, which, in Bandello's version, we see occur in Mantua.

39 In Shakespeare, there is an additional scene of violence when Paris comes upon Romeo at the graveyard. Count Paris tries to attack Romeo, thinking that he has come to defile Juliet's tomb, and Romeo kills him. This, of course, adds to the tragedy. This element is absent in Bandello.

40 In Shakespeare's version, Romeo has died before Juliet awakens, so we do not see their reunion, as we do here in Bandello's version.

41 Here we pick up the plot, broadly as it appears in Shakespeare's version.

42 Bandello draws in part here from a speech by Ghismonda, after the death of her love, in Boccaccio's Decameron, (Day 4, Story 1).

43 The Italian of this poem is a Petrarchan sonnet. The translation seeks to preserve meaning rather than poetic form.

Afterword

Having read to this point, some aspects of Matteo Bandello's novella will have already become clear in comparison to Shakespeare. Bandello's version is darker, for the issues of mental health (the melancholy of both Romeo and Juliet) drive the plot. They are not distracted from, as they are in Shakespeare's version.

Although Bandello wrote comedies as well as tragedies, there is nothing to relieve the gloom of his version of *Romeo and Juliet*. Not even the peace between the Montagues and Capulets, which is open-ended in Shakespeare's version, provides comfort for the loss of the two lovers in Bandello's story. The peace does not last and the killing starts again.

Bandello highlights the failure of all around them to save the two young people, suffering melancholy and driven to their deaths by societal forces they could not resist. Indeed, often the actions of those around them (pursuing sometimes interests and concerns other than the welfare of the two lovers) makes things worse. Friar Lawrence is a more self-interested and ambiguous character. Although fundamentally motivated by their daughter's wellbeing, Juliet's parents are impotent, misunderstanding their daughter, unable to communicate with her, and taking steps that lead to her death. Issues of youth suicide are still with us and if for nothing else, Bandello's version of *Romeo and Juliet* needs to be better known.

Yet, knowing Shakespeare's *Romeo and Juliet,* but not knowing the Matteo Bandello novella, is akin to Peter Jackson's *Lord of the Rings* without a J.R.R. Tolkien.

Romeo and Juliet is now one of the most loved and best-known dramas in the English language. It is still taught across the English-speaking world, and beyond (including in Shakespeare's version in Italy). Film adaptations of Romeo and Juliet appear regularly for new generations. It is no surprise that a story weaving together love and death with such poignancy should speak across cultural divides, as it did from the very beginning.

Although the setting and characters should make it obvious that the story is not originally from England, few, beyond scholars who study Shakespeare, know that he adapted the play from tales that appeared originally in Italy. Shakespeare's version is so successful that it is far better known than those of the Italian writers who first gave us the story, even in Italy.

Shakespeare in Love (Miramax, 1998), as mentioned in the Introduction, is one of the better adaptations of *Romeo and Juliet* to the screen, even if only loosely based on the play. The byline for the movie on IMDb gives a sense of how the movie is framed:

> *"The world's greatest ever playwright, William Shakespeare, is young, out of ideas and short of cash, but meets his ideal woman and is inspired to write one of his most famous plays."*[44]

From this premise, the movie takes us on an adventure through William Shakespeare's life and times, echoing the plot and scenes of *Romeo and Juliet,* and drawing on his other plays like *Twelfth Night,* with its cross-dressing, and *The Tempest,* with its shipwreck.

We get to enjoy Shakespeare's genius all over again, as Shakespeare experiences "real life" adventures in Elizabethan London. Different events "inspire" him, and, in his London garret, he feverishly pens *Romeo and Juliet,* entirely from his imagination. As a movie, it is brilliant and a great success, having won seven Oscars.

Of course, great art can't be constrained by history, but sadly, sometimes art holds history in contempt. In this case, the movie lost an opportunity to tell a deeper story about Shakespeare and to introduce its audience to great works of literature that delighted Shakespeare himself and that can delight us still, if we take the trouble to hunt them out.

AFTERWORD

There was no "ideal woman" in London who inspired Juliet. Not even a little bit. Juliet had already been written about in Italy by Matteo Bandello and those before him. As we have seen, she was a fully fleshed out character, whose actions and many of whose sentiments do not change between the Bandello and Shakespeare versions, although Shakespeare fashioned many beautiful new words for Juliet to say, which we do not find in the novella.

Although Shakespeare is enormously skilled and inventive in his use of language, writing both prose and poetry into his plays, he does not play fast and loose with his source material for this play. His version of *Romeo and Juliet* follows the plot of the story (as he knew it from the Brooke translation) quite faithfully. As Shakespeare was quite prepared to extensively modify other works for the stage, this tells us that the story was, in the main, already good enough.

We also discover that sometimes beautiful passages have been "lost in translation" between Bandello and Shakespeare. The translations on which Shakespeare relied were not always faithful to the original text, beginning with the French translation which was then re-translated into English.

Two entire scenes are lost that are so beautiful it is difficult to believe that, had he known about them, Shakespeare would have left them on the cutting room floor. One is Romeo's monologue when he believes Juliet to be dead, the other is the meeting between the two lovers at the Capulet tomb before they die in each other's arms. We can only wonder what Shakespeare's might have done with them. Such insights provide evidence that Shakespeare may never have read Bandello's Italian version, (although there is also evidence in the opposite direction).

Reading Bandello gives us new insights into Shakespeare's art. While he takes little away, he adds, enhancing the tragic and poignant beauty of the story.

The character Mercutio, who appears briefly in Bandello's version, is made a central character by Shakespeare. Mercutio's role in setting off the "curse" has already been mentioned in the Introduction. Dialogue like Mercutio's words: "Look for me tomorrow, Thou shalt find me a grave man," illustrates a tragicomedic element Shakespeare brings to the story. Figures such as Gregory and Sampson, who appear near the beginning of the play, also entertain the audience with their bawdy wit. They are stock characters taken from *commedia dell'arte,* which also made its way to England from Italy.

The brooding violence between the Capulet and Montague families is underlined by Shakespeare from the opening scene, and tension built until Tybalt's death. Near the end of the play, Shakespeare poignantly brings Count Paris and Romeo together beside Juliet's resting place (where they both mourn her, believing her dead). Their meeting places Romeo in a position where he must, again, unwillingly take a life, as Paris, in ignorance, seeks to defend the body of the woman he believed he was to marry. Such elements further enhance the tragedy of the play.

We discover clues to Shakespeare's creative process. In Shakespeare, when Juliet is debating with herself whether to take the sleeping potion, the nurse is absent and Juliet is alone, so that Giulietta's thoughts in Bandello become Juliet's words on stage in Shakespeare. Shakespeare includes what is virtually a stage direction in words he gives Juliet:

"Nurse! What should she do here?
My dismal scene I needs must act alone."

The English translations available to Shakespeare had already made the plot change. We are left to wonder if Shakespeare had access to the Bandello version (the only one in which the nurse is present), or whether he independently considered placing the nurse in the scene, but rejected it. Such insights into Shakespeare we draw from reading Bandello.[45]

It is helpful to know a little more about the context of Bandello's *Romeo and Juliet*. He wrote his version as a novella, which is a story longer than a short story but about a quarter the length of the modern-day novel. In the case of his *Romeo and Juliet*, it is around 15,300 words.[46]

The novella form was enormously popular before the invention of the novel, which did not appear in English until the late eighteenth century.

We can perhaps better understand the novella form if we remember that reading, in the past, wasn't necessarily a solitary activity. Often, books were read out loud in company, and in the absence of modern entertainment we now take for granted, it could be a wonderful way to pass an afternoon or evening together.

In fact, in the preamble written by Bandello (which is not reproduced here), it is exactly on such an occasion that he claims to have *heard* the story of *Romeo and Juliet* from a certain Captain Alessandro Pellegrino (a native of Verona) who told the story to a gathering at the house of a nobleman. When the tale begins we are hearing the voice of the Captain telling the story to the gathering (although this was a literary fiction).

We see the same pattern in Boccaccio's *Decameron*, which is a set of novellas framed by the gathering of a group of young men and women fleeing the plague who pass the time by telling such stories to each other, although the stories are oral rather than written.

Bandello's *Romeo and Juliet* can be read in an hour or two. He wrote more than 200 such novellas, with *Romeo and Juliet* as the ninth story in the second volume of his novellas. His novellas taken up by Shakespeare include: *Cymbeline, Much Ado About Nothing, Romeo and Juliet,* and *Twelfth Night*. Bandello's life story and influence as a writer is further outlined in *About the Author.*

In Italian there is a pithy phrase which captures the complexities of translation and which resonates better in Italian than it does in English: *traduttore traditore.* A translator is a traitor to the original.

In this translation, I wished to remain (as far as possible) faithful to Bandello's version and for his voice to carry through into the English phrases. Bandello's language is a beautiful, antiquated, but direct and clear Italian,[47] which translates very well to an English that we might find in stories about the Middle Ages.

At the same time, I have avoided introducing antiquated vocabulary or Shakespearean era language, so as to remain accessible to the modern reader. Generally, the result has been a translation that often draws directly on the words and phrases used by Bandello, although sometimes it is necessary to substitute language that flows more naturally in an English context.

The task of translating this work has been informed by my experience as a native speaker of Italian (which, together with Neapolitan, surrounded me as I grew up), by long reading in Italian in more recent years, and by my love of English literature. Italian (which was largely a written language for many centuries) has not altered as much as English since Matteo Bandello's time. I do not have formal training as a translator, but words and their use has been my daily task as a lawyer for many years and writing my preferred pastime, whenever time has allowed.

I was also encouraged to attempt this task, by the delight which I drew from my first foray into translating Italian literature. This was the translation in 2022 of *Il Drago,* a short story written by Luigi Capuana of the nineteenth century Sicilian *verismo* movement. I was often moved as I worked closely with the words and thoughts of the author. It is a peculiar quality of the written word that it speaks from mind to mind across chasms of space and time. Translation, somehow, makes the words manifest, almost as if the characters and happenings are come to life in the moment of translation. The same experience has attended translating Bandello's Romeo and Juliet. As the meaning of the Italian took shape in new English words the story's moments of romance leapt out in all their beauty and humanity and its tragedies, became heartrending as if Romeo and Juliet are really with us. And of course, in a sense they are. For the characters created by writers are not figments of the imagination, they are crystallizations of countless human experiences represented in story. I hope the reader will forgive any shortcomings they may find in this labour of love.

Bandello's words have a poignancy that strikes deep into the heart, when we allow ourselves to be carried along by his storytelling. It seemed important to seek to preserve that depth of feeling in English translation. The result, hopefully, conveys to an English-speaking audience something of the beauty and depth of emotion that Bandello's words carry.

A feeling of familiarity, from an *English-speaking viewpoint*, which I experienced reading Bandello, is perhaps no accident. There was indeed a shared literary culture across late Medieval and Renaissance Europe that even influenced the shape of the words and phrases we see in English literature. Italian stories are embedded in those of England and vice versa, as we can see in many examples.

The story of Lancelot and Guinevere shows up in Canto V of Dante's *Inferno,* with the tragic deaths of Paolo and Francesca. The book that tempted them to their eternal doom was known and read throughout Europe.

When Alessandro Manzoni set out to write the first "modern novel" for the Italian language in the early nineteenth century, the models that influenced him were those of the English Romantic writers, like Walter Scott's *Ivanhoe.*

In Shakespeare's time, the flow was very powerfully from Italian (then on the tail of the Renaissance) into English. Indeed, John Florio, an influential Italian writer in Elizabethan London, who wrote the earliest substantial Italian-English dictionary, contributed around 1100 words to the English language. He was the third most prolific contributor after Chaucer (c. 2000) and Shakespeare (c. 1900).

Shakespeare wasn't the only Elizabethan author to take up Italian stories. They were all the rage in Elizabethan England. Even if we go back to Chaucer, we find that he drew on the stories which Giovanni Boccaccio had collected in the *Decameron*.

These connections in storytelling were in part also drawn from the custom of travelers from England going on a "Grand Tour" of Europe, a tour that often ended in Italy, where its culture and ways were soaked up and later carried back home.

If you have, as I, drawn pleasure from discovering this older telling of *Romeo and Juliet,* there is much more to explore. Two earlier Italian versions of *Romeo and Juliet* are known in the decades before Bandello. One was written by Luigi Da Porto, who first placed the story in Verona. He was himself from Vicenza, not far from Verona. It is from Da Porto's version that we know that Bandello did not primarily work from an oral story he heard in a gathering. Rather he took Da Porto's text and expanded and made it better.

Even earlier, is the version by Masuccio Salernitano, which takes place in Siena and Egypt and in which Romeo and Juliet are named Mariotto and Gianozza. English translations are available of both these versions.[48]

As far as Bandello is concerned, his novellas contain other gems. The *Shakespeare Begins* series of translations will include his versions of *Twelfth Night* and *Much Ado About Nothing.* However, he was not the only Italian writer whose works graced Shakespeare's adaptations. In particular, there are those of the writer known in English as Cinthio, two of whose stories became Shakespeare's *Othello* and *Measure for Measure.*

Cinthio's tales are especially weighty, dealing with gender relations within the context of murder, domestic violence, manipulation, betrayal, sexual exploitation, and other issues. These themes still demand our attention and Renaissance writers made an important contribution to conversations that continue to this day. Cinthio's *Othello* and *Measure for Measure* will also appear as part of the *Shakespeare Begins* Series.

Finally, as we are concerned with *origins,* some discussion is called for on a minority theory of Shakespeare that has existed at the margins of traditional scholarship for centuries. That theory is known as the *Shakespeare authorship question.* Above, we have proceeded on the assumptions of traditional scholarship, which is perfectly adequate for most purposes.

Having read Bandello, there is no doubt that Shakespeare was not the author of the plot of *Romeo and Juliet.* In a sense, this already goes to the question of authorship.

Yet even in the case of the English versions of *Romeo and Juliet,* there are questions that illustrate why it is important to take the minority case seriously (despite the disdain sometimes heaped on it by traditional scholarship).

As discussed above, Brooke's version is usually seen as the primary *English* template for Shakespeare's play, but this is not the whole story. Brooke himself mentions that he was inspired to write his English translation after *seeing* a play of *Romeo and Juliet* performed. Earlier versions of the play were circulating in England before the later Shakespeare version with which we are familiar.[49]

The character of "Pietro" or "Balthasar" raises another source complication. In Shakespeare, "Peter" is a servant in Juliet's household, rather than in that of Romeo. This is in fact how the story was told by Luigi Da Porto, although not Bandello, on whom Brooke relies. Bandello had changed that plot point. In short, the play that has come down to us also seems to draw on the Italian text of the Da Porto version of the story, although no English translation is known to have been available in Shakespeare's time, and Shakespeare is not believed to have known Italian.[50]

Brooke moreover made many additions to the story, drawing for example on Chaucer's *Troilus and Cressida*. It is obvious when reading Bandello that Shakespeare, with some notable exceptions, strips away Brooke's modifications. In short, the Shakespeare text we have does not follow Brooke where his contribution is poor. Munro states:

> *"... that Shakspere used Brooke most where his version coincided with the older and unknown source ... It is important to notice how completely the faults which disfigure Brooke's work are absent from that of Shakspere."*[51]

The source Munro cites here is most likely the lost play (referenced by Brooke himself) on which Shakespeare seems to have placed considerable weight, knowing it to be closer to the original Italian sources.

When "Shakespeare's" *Romeo and Juliet* was first published decades later in 1597 (as the first quarto), it was published anonymously. When it was reworked in 1599, Shakespeare again does not claim authorship. The republication simply notes that it has been "newly corrected, augmented and amended." This also occurred in 1609, with the printing of the *third quarto*. It is only with the fourth quarto in 1622 that "written by W. Shake-speare" is added.

It is beyond the scope of this work to enter into the details of the authorship question. However briefly, it refers to the doubts that have persisted for centuries as to whether the Shakespeare of Stratford-upon-Avon was the true (or substantial) author of the plays attributed to him.

I will simply note the work of two recent authors, who in my view have made notable contributions to the debate.[52]

The first is Diana Price's peer reviewed work *Shakespeare's Unorthodox Biography, New Evidence of an Authorship Problem* (2013). It makes a case that deserves to be taken seriously. Price focuses specifically on the question of the documentary evidence during Shakespeare's own lifetime from people who personally knew the Shakespeare of Stratford supporting a conclusion that he was a writer, comparing him with the evidence available for contemporary playwrights. She concludes that unlike those contemporaries, virtually no evidence from Shakespeare's lifetime exists supporting that conclusion, although he undoubtedly had a hand in the production of the plays which are attributed to him, as a theatrical entrepreneur and perhaps in other ways.

Even more notable are the findings of Dennis McCarthy, who like Diana Price is an independent scholar. His work, and that of his colleagues, are reported by Michael Blanding in *North by Shakespeare: A Rogue Scholar's Quest for the Truth Behind Shakespeare* (Hachette Books, 2013), and in McCarthy's own growing list of publications including *Thomas North: The Original Author of the Shakespeare Plays* (2022) and in Mcarthy D. and Schlueter J., *Thomas North's 1555 Travel Journal: From Italy to Shakespeare* (Fairleigh Dickinson University Press, 2021).

In essence, McCarthy has used the techniques of plagiarism software to discover hundreds of previously unknown linguistic parallels between the writings of Sir Thomas North (1535-c.1604) and those of Shakespeare.

It has always been known that Shakespeare's Roman tragedies closely followed North's translation of *Plutarch's Lives,* lifting North's passages virtually verbatim, but the new parallels McCarthy has found span much of the dramatic corpus that is identified with Shakespeare. The borrowings that he identifies include not only the published works of North, but also his private unpublished papers and marginalia.

North himself is highly regarded for his prose writing which has been described as Shakespearean. McCarthy is of the view that North was the author of the play which Brooke saw before he penned the earliest *surviving* English version of *Romeo and Juliet*. Brooke and North were indeed both students at the Inns of Court where the play is reported, at around the relevant time. Shakespeare, however, had yet to be born.

An element I identified in the Introduction, as absent from Bandello but present in Shakespeare, was the moving juxtaposition of immediate transition from "wedding feast" to "funeral" when Juliet's family believe her to be dead.

Although this appears also in Brooke's version, McCarthy has established that the juxtaposition comes in fact from the pen of North many years before Shakespeare's *Romeo and Juliet* appeared in print. North created the juxtaposition in a poem in his translation of the *Dial of Princes* (1557). That juxtaposition, McCarthy discovers was copied by both Brooke and Shakespeare. He notes also the suggestive fact that North travelled to Italy (including passing through Mantua and nearby Verona) with a Viscount Montague[53] in 1555. It is this form of the Montecchi name that appears in Shakespeare's *Romeo and Juliet* and in Brooke's version, possibly both from the original lost play which McCarthy attributes to North.McCarthy achieves similar insights across the Shakespeare canon, noting that the existence of earlier versions of "Shakespeare" plays (most now lost) is not uncommon.

At a minimum, we must conclude that Shakespeare was profoundly influenced by North through long and close personal association with him and his works, or as McCarthy maintains, that the source material for Shakespeare's *Romeo and Juliet* and other plays which are considered "Shakespearean" were largely provided by North to Shakespeare. McCarthy however does not exclude that Shakespeare's hand also contributed to texts of the plays, once received in that way. McCarthy, indeed, appears to have solved the authorship question.[54]

As may be imagined, the debate around the authorship question is heated and sometimes less courteous than it ought be. Shakespeare is a venerated figure. Like other national figures, what happens to him *matters*. For English-speakers, he is connected with our sense of identity.

The debate (although not in a scientific field), has all the hallmarks of a "scientific revolution" of the kind described by Thomas Kuhn: committed defenders of orthodoxy facing off against proponents of a new and radically different paradigm for better understanding some aspect of reality. The camps struggle to speak to each other, for they live in different conceptual worlds.[55] Sometimes, sadly, this is how understanding advances.

There is no doubt of the existence of a William Shakespeare who was a successful participant in the Elizabethan theatre. The plays are, of course, traditionally attributed to Shakespeare and his name appears on the *First Folio*. Further, through natural ability and long participation in theatrical companies, he could have grown to become a talented writer, as he is famed to be.

Yet, his works clearly drew on the writings of others. This is not questioned by anyone who has seriously looked at the source history of his plays. Nor was this unusual in Shakespeare's era. Taking earlier works and making them better (including claiming authorship) was a popular literary pastime. When we see how *Romeo and Juliet* improved through this very practice, we have to wonder if perhaps the writers of this era were onto something. The demand that a great writer be largely or entirely original is a modern conceit. Nonetheless, it raises the question of how much of Shakespeare's work was his own. There is something to be said for getting to as much of the historical truth as we can. After all, my motivation in working on this translation was at least in part to make the historical truth of Bandello's work and the origins of Shakespeare's *Romeo and Juliet* better known.

Regardless of where the debate lands in the end, we can see the value of theories like those of Dennis McCarthy as lenses for better understanding the Shakespearean works we love. The myths of *Shakespeare in Love* dissipate and in their place we trace the outlines of how the works of Bandello and his peers in Italy took shape in a new form in the English canon.

Moreover, we have seen in this translation that Bandello was not the source of Shakespeare's style. Based on McCarthy's work, we find that style instead, in significant measure, in the prose works of Sir Thomas North. Shakespeare was profoundly influenced by him. Another piece of the puzzle falls into place.

What we can be certain of is that there was a whole milieu in Elizabethan high society in cultural dialogue with Italy. That milieu was both the laboratory and primary audience of the literary innovations that swept England in this era. Elizabeth I, herself, was proficient in Italian, having been taught the language by her Italian tutor Giovanni Battista Castiglione. It is to this milieu, directly or indirectly, that we owe Shakespeare's remarkable plays, including *Romeo and Juliet*. And if we would know the origins even further, whether in England or beyond, our explorations will take us to the writers of the Italian Renaissance, not least, to the remarkable works of Matteo Bandello.

If a criticism might be made of the enormous literature in English about the origins of Shakespeare, it is the frequent omission or minimization of the written Italian source materials when discussing the plays. Many of those sources are still very much available today and are the foundations upon which the plays are elaborated.

A partial excuse is found in the challenges of approaching literature in a different language. I hope in producing this new translation of Matteo Bandello's *Romeo and Juliet,* his delightful prose may become more accessible to interested scholars and students of

AFTERWORD

Shakespeare, as well as to readers who simply want to enjoy a great story, well-told.

I hope also that this translation demonstrates that we cannot really understand how Shakespeare worked, or his contribution, without knowing the source material.

It is sometimes said that Homer was not one poet, but many, whose contributions were all captured under the magic and myth of his name. We can reach the same conclusions about Shakespeare. The works of Shakespeare are a palimpsest. The original tales and ideas were written over by generation after generation of writers. In the case of *Romeo and Juliet* writers in Italy, France, and England are all part of that beautiful story. To the mythic name Shakespeare we must add (to cite just the principal players) Brooke, North, Boaistuau, and in Italy, Bandello, Da Porto and Masuccio Salernitano. Today, we would regard such writers as co-authors of the final product.

Michael Curtotti
Canberra/Ngambri/Ngunnawal
June 30th, 2023

---

44 Internet Movie Database entry for *Shakespeare in Love* accessed December 2022 https://www.imdb.com/title/tt0138097/

45 Other indications that Shakespeare may have read Bandello, are the use of the term "stoccata" and the name "Benvolio." See notes 16 and 24, above.

46 The first quarto of *Romeo and Juliet* published in England in 1597 amounts to around 19,500 words. The Arden edition (based primarily on the second quarto of 1599) is around 25,700 words.

47 Despite Bandello's significance and influence beyond Italy, in Italy itself his Italian was in the past criticized for its departure from the strictures of Florentine. Defining himself a native of Lombardy, he modestly professes not to have mastered a Florentine style. His Italian is no more challenging than that of Boccaccio to a modern reader. Of course, such linguistic standards are rather arbitrary and his departures do not detract from his skill as a master storyteller.

48 At time of writing, the Skenè Research Centre of the University of Verona, maintains an annotated digital text of Bandello's *Romeo and Juliet* which is cross referenced with accessible passages from Da Porto and French and English translations and adaptations of Matteo Bandello's tale, including Shakespeare's first and second quartos of *Romeo and Juliet*. *https:// skene.dlls.univr.it/en/bandello-modernised/*

49 We may note also the stream of references to Romeo or Romeus and Juliet or Juliet in English Elizabethan literature including in the years 1565, 1574, 1576 - 1580, and 1582 - 1584. Romeo and Juliet were already among the most famous lovers in English literature. See Early English Books online https://quod.lib.umich.edu/e/eebogroup/

AFTERWORD

---

50 On this question, see discussion in Chapter 11 of Moore, Olin Harris. *The Legend of Romeo and Juliet*. Ohio State University Press, 1950. Olin's book provides an excellent history of the evolution of *Romeo and Juliet* across Europe.

51 Munro, James (ed). Brooke's *"Romeus and Juliet": Being the Original of Shakespeare's "Romeo and Juliet"*. Vol. 3. Humphrey Milford, Oxford University Press, 1908, pp xlv-lv

52 The debate around the authorship question is vast, although definitively "unorthodox." I will simply note that a candidate most often put forward by many as the "true author of the plays" has been Edward de Vere, Earl of Oxford. The fictional movie *Anonymous* (2011), is based on that theory.

53 In the first quarto version of Romeo and Juliet (1597), the name is rendered "Mountague."

54 The preceding discussion draws largely from Dennis McCarthy, *Thomas North: The Original Author of the Shakespeare Plays* (2022), particularly chapter 9 and Appendix G. See also de Wolf Fuller, Harold. "Romeo and Juliette." *Modern Philology* 4, no. 1 (1906): 75-120, which argues that the original source play was preserved in a Dutch translation from c. 1630. In his introduction, Munro, op. cit. p 139, also reaches the conclusion that the Dutch play may well have been based on an earlier play which was also a source for the Shakespeare play.

55 Chalmers, Alan F. *What is this thing called science?*. Hackett Publishing, 2013, contains an accessible summary of Thomas Kuhn's insights.

Table of Characters

Shakespeare	Bandello	Role
Romeo Montague	Romeo Montecchio	Main protagonist
Juliet Capulet	Giulietta Capelletto	Main protagonist
Nurse	An old woman/wet nurse	Juliet's servant
Balthasar	Pietro	A Servant to Romeo
Mercutio	Marcuccio	Romeo's friend
Benvolio	(Unnamed)	Romeo's friend
Balthasar	-	Servant to Romeo
Escalus	Bartolomeo della Scala	Prince of Verona
Capulet	Antonio Capelletto	Head of the Capulets
Lady Capulet	Madonna Giovanna	Wife of Capulet
Montague	Montecchio	Head of the Montagues
Lady Montague	-	Wife of Montague
Tybalt	Tebaldo	Nephew of Capulet
Count Paris	Il conte Paris	Juliet's unwanted fiancé
Peter	-	A servant of the Capulets
Friar Lawrence	Fra Lorenzo	A Franciscan friar

TABLE OF CHARACTERS

Shakespeare	Bandello	Role
Friar John	Fra Anselmo	Commissioned to deliver a message to Romeo
An Apothecary	An unnamed snake charmer of Spoleto	Provides poison to Romeo
Sampson	-	A servant to Capulet
Gregory	-	A servant to Capulet
Abram	-	A servant to Montague

Scene Index

The table below provides a cross-reference between Matteo Bandello's text and the acts and scenes of Shakespeare's *Romeo and Juliet* (Arden edition) together with a brief explanation of how the plot of the two versions compare. Bandello's text is referenced by Act numbers, capital letters, and page numbers, corresponding to the relevant scene or parts of scenes. Sections that do not appear in Shakespeare are noted and vice versa.

Act One

Bandello	Shakespeare	Outline
p1	Prologue	Both texts introduce fair Verona and the tragic lovers. In Shakespeare, the prologue is also used to introduce the conflict between the two great houses.
1A, p3	Scene I	Bandello outlines the conflict between the two houses and the efforts of the Prince to suppress it. Shakespeare dramatizes these themes through the comic characters Sampson and Gregory, introducing characters such as Romeo, Benvolio, Tybalt, the Prince, and the Capulets.

SCENE INDEX

Bandello	Shakespeare	Outline
1B, p3	Scene II	Bandello's narrative explores Romeo's melancholy at length and his love for a certain "gentle lady," which his friends counsel him to abandon. They urge him to go to the Capulet ball. Shakespeare covers this in his Scene II, but in a more comic and summary vein.
-	Scene III	This scene appears only in Shakespeare and dwells on the efforts of Juliet's mother to marry off Juliet. In Bandello's novella, Juliet's parents only think of having her married as a way to solve her worrisome and unexplained melancholy. Juliet's unwillingness to marry appears in both versions, but remains unexplained in Shakespeare. In Bandello, Juliet is already married to Romeo at the time of this conversation, which happens later in the plot.
-	Scene IV	Shakespeare introduces the character of Mercutio, whose comic and tragic elements are well developed. Mercutio delivers his Queen Mab monologue. In Bandello, "Marcuccio" only appears at the Capulet ball, although his humorous nature is already introduced.

SCENE INDEX

Act Two

Bandello Shakespeare Outline

-	Prologue	In Shakespeare, the chorus dwells on the difficulties before the two lovers.
2A, p11	-	In Bandello, we see Juliet in turmoil, laying in her bed and wondering about Romeo's love for her and whether it may be trusted. Romeo, meanwhile, visits her window daily to catch a glimpse of her.
-	Scene I	In Shakespeare, Benvolio and Mercutio are unable to find their friend Romeo, who has disappeared into Juliet's garden.
2B, p12	Scene II	In this balcony scene, both texts show Romeo and Juliet having their first conversation. They declare their love, and in both, Juliet rejects Romeo's request to come up to her room, but he accepts her request for marriage. Here, Shakespeare is far more poetic than Bandello, introducing some of his most memorable verses.
2C, p14	Scene III	In both versions, Romeo meets with Friar Lawrence (and we learn of his skill in alchemy and potions). Friar Lawrence agrees to marry the pair in secret. In Bandello, Friar Lawrence hopes to win greater favor with the Prince by reconciling the two houses.

SCENE INDEX

Act Three

Bandello	Shakespeare	Outline
3A, p19	-	In Bandello, Romeo and Juliet meet in Juliet's garden and consummate their marriage. They plan to reconcile their houses. This scene is absent in Shakespeare, but replaced in Act III, Scene V, when he has couple parting, after, by implication, having consummated the marriage.
3B, p20	Scene I	In Bandello, Friar Lawrence also makes efforts to reconcile the houses. In both texts, a chance encounter in the streets of Verona between Montagues and Capulets leads to death. In Shakespeare, Mercutio dies and curses both houses. In both versions, Romeo tries to stop the fighting, but ends up killing Tybalt. In Bandello, Romeo acts in self-defense. In Shakespeare, he is driven to seek revenge for the death of Mercutio. In both versions, the Prince banishes Romeo.
3C, p22	Scene II	In Bandello, there is great mourning in the Capulet household and Juliet secretly meets with Romeo, offering to escape with him dressed as a boy, but Romeo discourages her, seeking another solution. In Shakespeare, the scene focuses solely on Juliet's distress about Romeo having killed Tybalt.

SCENE INDEX

Bandello	Shakespeare	Outline
3D, p24	Scene III	In Bandello, Romeo departs for Mantua. Juliet becomes depressed, seeing no hope of ever being with Romeo. They exchange letters and Romeo tries to cheer her heart. In Shakespeare, we see Romeo being counseled in Friar Lawrence's cell and a visit from Juliet's nurse, who reports Juliet's distress and brings Romeo a ring from her.
3E, p25	Scenes IV & V	In Shakespeare, Capulet meets again with Paris and decides that Paris and Juliet are to be married in a few days. In Bandello, Romeo has left and Juliet's parents become increasingly concerned as they cannot understand her continual weeping and sadness. Her mother imagines it is because she is unmarried and consults her husband to have her married. Capulet strikes upon a marriage with Count Paris. In Shakespeare, Romeo and Juliet meet again before he departs for Mantua at her balcony. It is implied that they have consummated the marriage at this point. In both versions, Juliet argues with her father, refusing to marry, but is, in both cases, told she must. In Shakespeare, Juliet uses double entendre (which the audience understands), at the same time hiding the truth from her parents and declaring her secret love.

Act Four

SCENE INDEX

Bandello	Shakespeare	Outline
-	Scene IV	In Shakespeare, we see final preparations for the wedding feast. This assists Shakespeare's transition from wedding to funeral–from joy to grief–in the space of hours. This scene is not present in Bandello.
4D, p37	Scene V	In both versions the nurse finds Juliet dead in her bed and the house falls to grief. In Shakespeare, this dramatic moment is underlined, as wedding feast immediately becomes funeral. In Bandello, it is dramatized by the suffering of Juliet's mother.
4E, p39	-	In Bandello, Friar Lawrence writes to Romeo, explaining the plan, and sends a trusted friar to Mantua to deliver the message. Due to an outbreak of plague, he is unable to deliver the message to Romeo. In Shakespeare, we do not witness the friar's journey, but later hear his report to Friar Lawrence that he has failed to deliver his message due to an outbreak of pestilence.
4F, p40	Scene V continued	In Bandello, Juliet is buried in the tomb, with Friar Lawrence officiating and placing her next to Tybalt. In Shakespeare, Friar Lawrence arrives at the Capulet house to comfort the grieving family, but we do not see Juliet buried.

Act Five

SCENE INDEX

About the Author

Matteo Bandello is one of the greatest storytellers of the Renaissance. He has been described as the second most influential Italian novelist after Boccaccio. His works and their adaptations, have been enjoyed across Europe; influencing writers such as Byron, Cervantes, Lope de la Vega, Stendhal and not least Shakespeare. His writings have been in publication in multiple languages across the centuries since he originally wrote them. Shakespeare was just one of those who adapted his stories to the stage. Bandello's personal life is as fascinating as the stories he tells. Although coming from a wealthy family, he was sent to a life in the church for which he seems to have been unsuited. Instead, his greatest passion was writing. Born in 1480 in Piedmont, he spent his early years in Milan, Mantua and Verona. His privileged life was interrupted by the endemic warfare of his time, which made him a refugee for the remainder of his life. In 1525, war came to his family home. His library and manuscripts were lost or stolen. He fled, wandering about Italy. Eventually he was forced to leave it all together. His new home was France, and in 1550, the King of France appointed him Bishop of Agen. During this last period of his life he was able to collect his manuscripts and complete his literary works, leaving church administration to others. His stories first appeared in print in 1554, quickly establishing him as one of the most well-known writers of Europe.

About the Translator

Michael Curtotti is a writer and practicing lawyer. His first translation was *The Dragon the Witch and the Daughters* by Luigi Capuana (Aldila Press, 2023, 2022), a delightful tale of the transformation worked in the life of an old man by two orphans, written by a master of the nineteenth century *verismo* movement. Currently Michael is working on a translation of Cinthio's *Othello* and other Italian stories Shakespeare adapted to the stage. In 2022, Michael edited *Dante Under the Southern Cross 2021: Australian Reflections for the 700th Anniversary of the Passing of Dante Alighieri (Dante Alighieri Society Canberra, 2022)*. In 2020, Michael published *Ten Lives Declaring Human Rights: From Bartolomeo de Las Casas to Martin Luther King Jr.* (Aldila Press, 2020), a series of short biographies which tell the story of human rights. He has written over 340 articles and over half a million words on his writer's website titled *Beyond Foreignness* at https://beyondforeignness.org. Michael was born in Italy and grew up in Australia. He is married with three children. He speaks English and Italian and is an enthusiastic student of Arabic, a language he one day hopes to master.

Acknowledgements

Writing (or indeed translating) a book is not undertaken alone. There are many who help along the way. Greatest thanks of course are due to my family who have been a constant support and who bear with the writerly absence; that unavoidable companion of the creative process, especially my wife and beloved, Ranjana, to whom this book is dedicated. I would also like to the thank my readers who give me hope that these endeavors are worthwhile, especially to Fran who is supporting a special event on mental health and the arts which is planned for next year. Also, to the professionals who have helped me in preparing this book for publication: Peter Selgin who created the cover design, Maria Scala who undertook an extensive copy and structural edit of an earlier version of this work, Jessie Cunniffe who developed, in discussion with me, the book description and last but not least Azzurra Cirrincione for proofreading and editing the Italian translation of the Introduction and the backmatter. Dennis McCarthy kindly reviewed a draft of the section of the Afterword describing his work on Sir Thomas North. Thank you also to David Curry, a lifelong friend, who on our walks together has provided unfailing encouragement and insights and for his wonderful support with marketing this book. Franco Papandrea and Eloisa and Faustino Troni also for their kindness in reviewing and improving the Italian of the Introduction and Afterword. Also to Paul Murphy who very kindly undertook a thorough proofreading of a final draft of the English text and Francesco Ricatti who gave me an opportunity to share this translation with his students of Italian at the Australian National University. Finally to the small band of Canberra writers whose meetings and presence provide collegial support and inspiration. Thank you to each and every one of you, and to many others who have helped me in different ways. Although writing is often a solitary undertaking, strangely it also leads us to discover new and treasured friendships.

www.ingramcontent.com/pod-product-compliance
Lightning Source LLC
Chambersburg PA
CBHW051307170626
46809CB00004B/1787